Liam

The *Devil Souls* Motorcycle Club

LeAnn Ashers

dedication

To my readers. You have been begging for Liam and Paisley since my "Forever" series. You have gotten your wish. <3

LeAnn Ashers

prologue

Paisley

Oh my goodness, could he get any more beautiful? We have a new boy at school named Liam, and he is absolutely gorgeous, the kind of good looks that take your breath away. He started school about a week ago, and he keeps to himself.

He has this bad boy look that is killing my soul. He has dark brown hair that is slightly longer on top and swept to the side. His eyes are a beautiful dark brown, and they watch my every move.

From the moment he saw me, his eyes have never left me. He just watches me. I do not understand why. At first I thought I had food smudged on my mouth or a stain on my clothes. That is not the case; he just watches me, and I haven't gotten the nerve to speak to him yet. So ball-less me just lowers her head, blushing, and goes on with her day. Girls flock around him, but he just ignores them. I've decided I am going to introduce myself to him tomorrow. God, I am such a spaz! Why can't I just talk to him? Be brave, Paisley!

My phone buzzes in my pocket, and I see a text from my father. He will be able to pick me up early. I grab my bag off the bleachers. I have P.E. this period, and we are just sitting around doing nothing. They won't even notice I am gone.

Sneaking out the door, I peek back to make sure that the teacher isn't looking, and she is on her phone as usual. I shoot a text to Dad letting him know I will be waiting for him outside. He messages back instantly: Okay.

My father has raised me by himself, and I couldn't ask for a better dad. I may not have had a mother, but he went above and beyond. I also have my uncles, the guys who were around for my first day of school and, when I started playing sports, came to all of my games. They may not look like the kind of men who would play dress-up and have tea parties—they have a hard and mean exterior—but on the inside they are soft, at least when it comes to certain things.

That is family.

As I'm walking out the front door, I hear something hit the floor behind me. I peek back to see the weird janitor everyone at school avoids. He grins at me, sets his mop against the wall, and walks toward me. I duck out the door and hurry around the side of the building, hoping I lose him.

I wonder if Liam is interested in me. I've never even had a boyfriend before, let alone kissed a guy. My dad scared away any guy who dared to look twice at me, and don't get me started on my uncles.

"Well, if it isn't Paisley."

Fear shoots up my spine and goose bumps break out across my skin.

"What are you doing?" My voice shakes and my palms are sweaty and trembling.

The feeling in my gut is telling me to run, but he is standing between me and the only exit. He continues to grin as he starts to unbutton his shirt. No. This is not happening right now. I am completely imagining this.

Instincts take over and, without thinking, I run toward the entrance to the alley. Fingers snatch my hair, throwing me to the ground, knocking the wind out of me. I am frozen with fear. He falls down beside me and reaches for my hands. I punch him hard in the face, and his head snaps back. I raise my fist again and he pins it above my head. He grins at me; his teeth are covered in blood. I punch him with my free hand and kick my legs, hoping and praying to dislodge him from me. He catches my left hand, pinning it beside the right one. His face bends toward mine, and I turn my head to the side, warm tears falling down my face. This is my worst fear, and it is happening right at school.

His warm breath fans across my face, making me gag. "Please don't do this." My heart hurts, and the terror fills every part of me with pain. *Why?*

He releases me with one hand and I try to pull free, but he grips both of my wrists with the other hand. I try to hit him with my knee, and he laughs right in my face. "Shh, it's okay." His finger trails down the side of my jaw. I swallow back the vomit and let out a deep heart-wrenching sob. "It's better to be broken in first before I turn you over to the guys to sell."

Sell. The word is thundering in my brain. I stare at the sky, the sun beaming down, and I plead with this man, begging him not to do that. Then his weight is torn off of me. I sob into my hands and, through blurry eyes, I see Liam beating him. I fall back, reeling from what just happened. A man just tried to... I sink my hands into my hair and pull it, hoping that I wake up from this horrible dream.

"Liam!" a woman yells, and I feel hands snaking under my body. I open my eyes to see his dark ones bearing down on me, his face filled with rage. I close my eyes once more, letting it sink in that I am safe.

He turns around and I hear a sound that will never leave me. "No!" Dad yells. Liam tightens his grip on me, and I take a step back. My dad calls the guys, telling them to get here and runs over, taking me from Liam. In that moment, breathing in the smell of my father and the sense of safety that he gives off in waves, the dam breaks. I cling to him, his arms tight around me. He is shaking just as hard as I am. "He will pay for this, Baby." He kisses the top of my head, and I close my eyes and cry against his chest.

I just want to go home. "Fuck." Dad lifts me off the ground, tucking me against him. I bury my face in his chest and let him shield me from the world. In this moment I am not a teenager, but a little girl again.

The guys arrive a few minutes later. Kyle walks up to us, and the others follow close behind. "Talk," Kyle says and Liam relays everything that happened.

I raise my head and mouth to Liam, "Thank you." He nods and goes back to talking to Kyle. A few minutes later Dad carries me to the car and I close my eyes, allowing sleep to take me.

Liam

Seventeen

That is a moment I will never fucking forget. The sight of her on the ground like that and someone wanting to hurt her will forever be stamped into my brain.

She is like an angel. She had my attention the moment I walked into the school. She smiled at everyone and floated around making everyone happy by just being in her presence. It was fucking intoxicating.

I want her, but I am not someone who can be the guy next door. I had a hard time and had to live rough until I moved in with my sister. I am the exact opposite of Paisley. I am dark, mean, and rough. I talk with my fists. She is light and happiness, too beautiful to be in this cold fucking place. That doesn't stop me from wanting her, but I settle for watching her and protecting her. Maybe someday, once I become the man she deserves, then I can have her. One thing is for certain, I am a determined motherfucker.

Paisley

A Week Later

It was finally time for me to go back to school. I don't think I will ever be ready, but it's time for me to move on with my life. So now I'm sitting at lunch, and all of my friends have completely abandoned me, leaving me all alone with people staring at me. They're looking at me like I am from a different planet. Nobody knows what happened except for the people I thought of as friends, but I guess they spread it around.

I duck my head and stare at the tray in front of me, my appetite completely gone. Them not being my friends isn't a big deal to me, not compared to everything else that happened. Someone sets down a tray directly beside me, and I look up to see Liam, much to my surprise. He sits down beside me and I stare at him. What is he doing? He begins opening my food and drink for me while I just stare.

He finally looks at me for the first time, a small smile tugging at the edges of his lips. I smile and lower my head again, blushing hard. He is so beautiful it's hard not to smile. I offer him my hand, like a dork. "Paisley."

He looks at my hand, his twitching lips turning into a full-blown smile. "Liam."

This was the start of my forever.

A Couple of Years Later

Paisley

Today is the day I have dreaded more than anything. Today is the day my best friend in the whole world is leaving for basic training. Liam is someone I have come to trust and care about. There is also a part of me that wants him. God, do I want him. I have this fear buried deep in my heart because I am scared for him. I am scared that he will be taken away from me. A knock on my bedroom door interrupts my fears, and Liam steps into my room.

"Sneaking in again?" I ask, a grin sliding over my face for the first time today. He winks, neither confirming nor denying. He shuts the door behind him, and my stomach sinks because he is such a beautiful man. I thought he was beautiful the first time I met him, but now? He has changed. He is taller, at least six foot five, his body has filled out, and he has a killer smile. I scoot across the bed so he can sit beside me. We watch TV together, as we have time and time again, but we won't do this again for a long time. I stare at the TV, not looking at him even though I can feel him staring at me, demanding that I look at him. I don't want him to see me cry.

"What happened?" he asks, and his hand wraps around mine. I don't say anything, and my throat tightens. He touches my jaw and turns my head to look at him. His eyes darken when he sees my tears, and his nose flares. "Who fucking bothered you?"

Bothered me? I close my eyes and laugh. I fall forward and lay my head on his chest while shaking with laughter.

"Paisley?" His hand is resting on the back of my head.

I push him away and smile up at him because he so cute. "Nobody bothered me."

He studies my face to make sure I am being truthful. "Why are you sad then?" He touches my jaw, wiping away a tear. He is a sweetheart.

"I am sad because you're leaving."

He closes his eyes, his hand in my hair. It's so quiet I can hear the clock ticking on the wall. His eyes slowly open, locking with mine. "I was going to tell you this shit tomorrow, but I am going to tell you now."

Oh my goodness, what could it be? He lifts me up and sets me down directly in front of him, with only a few inches separating our faces. His hand moves from my hair to the side of my face. "I have wanted you since the moment I met you, but I didn't want to claim you until I deserve you, and I realize that I will never deserve you, my love. I also knew that I never wanted you to wait for me to come back from basic, or while I am deployed. I want you to live your dreams and do whatever you want to do in life." He gives me that sexy smile. "But know that the moment I am done with the SEALs, I am coming for your ass."

Oh my fucking god. I narrow my eyes at him. "Well, I wish you had told me sooner because I would have done this a long time ago."

He gives me a questioning look, but I never stop to give him an answer. I lean forward, pressing my lips against his.

Heaven.

His hands are on my face, taking control of the kiss. His lips are soft as they move over mine in a way that I will never forget.

This is my first kiss.

A few minutes later, he slowly lets me go and presses his forehead against mine. "I have wanted that for so long," he whispers.

I will wait for him. I will live my life and start my career—I want to be a nurse—but I want him. "I will wait for you, Liam," I whisper, and I kiss his cheek and lie against his chest once more.

Liam

I feel fucking stupid. I thought for years that she could not want someone like me. I am the son of a prostitute and a man who spends his days beating up his wife. I started working the moment I was old enough, so I could eat. I was surrounded by pimps and guys paying my mother. Way too many times I saw her get her ass beat. I would step in the way and try to defend her. No matter how many times she did shitty things, she was still my mother. Then she was fucking killed.

Then I went to live with my father, who was an asshole, and I hate his fucking guts. His wife saw him beating my ass, so she left him, which shocked the shit out of me. I never expected that, nor did I expect her to say I had a sister. My sister had lived a fucked-up life just as I had.

My father's wife helped me sneak out in the middle of the night, and she took me to my sister. It was the best thing that had ever happened to me. My sister gave me a life I'd never imagined I would have. Then I became a prospect for the Devil Souls MC and found out what I was meant to do in life. That was when I met her, Paisley.

Paisley

No, no, no. Other guys around his age are climbing into the bus that will take him away from me. "Don't fucking do it," he warns, glaring at me because I am close to crying once more.

I roll my eyes, pushing him slightly. "Yeah, well, I would like to see you try to stop me," I tease.

That sexy slow smile slides over his face once more. He comes closer to me, and I brace myself. "I bet I could," he taunts, before he kisses me.

Right in front of my father, I grip Liam's shirt and kiss him back as hard as I can.

"What the fuck!" Dad yells.

He pulls back and kisses my forehead, his fingers intertwined with mine. "I will see you soon, remember what I said. The moment I am out."

I finish for him, looking into his eyes. "You're coming for me."

He hugs me once more then lets me go. I bite my lip as he climbs onto the bus, and he sits by the window directly in front of me. I put on a brave face and smile and he winks; then the bus is moving. Taking him away. This is just one chapter of many in our lives. He's wanted a military career since before I met him, and I would never deprive him of what he wants, but I don't want to see him go. I want him to follow his dreams. Just like he never wanted to act on his feelings for me because he didn't want me to follow him from base to base—he wanted me to achieve my dreams. He says I don't deserve him, but he is selfless and kind, the most amazing person I have ever met. I think I don't deserve him.

one

Eight Years Later

Paisley

I am dead on my feet; I just finished a twelve-hour shift. Now that I am clocked out, I look at my phone for the hundredth time in the last hour. Dad told me a few days ago that shit has gone down in the club and to be on my toes.

"I don't know about you, girl, but I am ready to pass out," my best friend Vanessa says. We walk into the locker room and grab our things.

"I am exhausted myself, girl, my feet are killing me." The emergency room has been absolutely bonkers today, and I haven't even gotten a chance to have lunch yet, so I am stopping at the local burger place and stuffing my face. Vanessa waits while I gather my things; then she pushes the door open and steps out—and freezes.

Fear shivers up my spine. "Vanessa?" I ask. I slide past her and follow her gaze.

My heart stops right then and there. He is leaning against the wall, across from the locker rooms. He is huge, tattooed, and beautiful.

He is my Liam.

"Oh my god!" I drop my stuff and he grins at me.

I haven't seen him since he was deployed two years ago. I knew he was getting close to being done, but I hadn't heard from him. I run to him, jump up, and wrap my arms and legs around him. His arms wrap around me tightly, his face pressed against mine.

"I have missed you so much," I whisper, hugging him tighter. You don't know how much you miss someone until the very moment he is back in your life. He has been my best friend since I was sixteen years old; I am now twenty-six.

"I missed you too."

I close my eyes and breathe in his scent. It wraps around me like a blanket, bringing warmth, protection. He sets me down on the ground, and I grin at Vanessa, who is looking from me to Liam with her mouth agape.

"This is Liam?" she asks.

I nod my head frantically, smiling up at him. "You're home now, right?" I ask him.

"I am."

Vanessa grins at me, because he is all I have talked about since she and I met. I can't help it. I look at him from the corner of my eye, and he is just beautiful.

Liam

I am home. After many years of being deployed and based here or there, I am finally home.

I was planning on stopping at the Grim Sinners' on the way back to the Devil Souls', because it was on the way, only to find out that the shit has hit the fan.

A cartel has moved in on the Grim Sinners, and they have already set up shop in Raleigh, my town. The Grim

Sinners caught one of the fuckers, so I took over doing what I fucking do best, getting information any and every way possible.

I learned that they had a plan to attack the women and kids of the club, threatening right where it hurts.

My first thought was *Paisley*. She is the princess of the Devil Souls; she was the only girl for many years. She lives alone. She would be the perfect person for them to go after first. Good fucking thing I am home, because touching her is the last thing they will ever do.

"Bye guys!" her friend says and walks down the hallway, leaving me and Paisley alone. She looks at me, excited.

"I can't believe you're home," she whispers.

"I am." I touch her jaw, smiling down at her. I have not fucking smiled like this in years; the only time I do is when I am around her.

Fuck me, isn't she beautiful?

I have waited eight years to be home, and I am going to do this shit right—the way it's supposed to be—like this is the first time I have met her.

Paisley

He is Liam, but I can also tell he is different. Every single time I have seen him over the years, he has seemed different. He is aware of everything around him—his eyes looking at everything around us—ready for an attack.

"I drove my bike, I will follow you to wherever you want to eat."

We walk out of the hospital to the dark parking lot. Liam puts his hand on the small of my back, pressing me into his side without a second thought.

Just like he used to.

I know it's going to take a while to get used to him being home; it's been eight years. He used to be my best friend—we were inseparable—but things are not the same. It's not like we can go back eight years. Things are different; I am different and he is different.

I click the clicker to my car, and the lights turn on inside. He opens my door and I step inside and start the car.

"I will be behind you." He shuts the door, leaving me to stare at his receding back.

Okay, what happens next? I throw my purse on the passenger seat and, as I'm pulling out, I hear the roar of his bike. My taillights give his face an eerie red glow that makes him look like a mean motherfucker.

Oh boy.

I arrive at the burger place a few minutes later, and he pulls up beside me. Before I've turned off the ignition, he is opening my door.

My phone rings, and I answer it. "Hey, Dad."

"Hey baby girl, I guess you know who's home?" Dad grumbles unhappily.

I roll my eyes because he has always pretended to dislike Liam, but we all know he secretly likes him. Liam saved me when I was sixteen, and Dad has never forgotten that.

Neither have I; that day is one I will never forget.

"Yeah, he's here."

Liam leans against my open door, his arms across his chest.

"Baby, shit is going down with the clubs. Tell Liam to let you in on everything. Love you, sweetheart." He hangs up the phone.

I look at Liam. "Dad told me to tell you to let me in on everything that is going on."

He rubs his face and looks up at the sky, frustrated. "I will tell you once we get back to your house."

Wait.

Did he say *my house*?

"My house?"

A slow grin comes over his face, that same sexy grin that I loved seeing when we were teenagers. "Did I not mention I am staying with you?"

I raise a hand. "Hold the fuck up…" I start and he laughs, takes my raised hand, and pulls me from the car. "Shit is going down, like your dad said." He brings his face closer to mine, a smile tugging at his lips. "That means you're to be protected." He stops, looking highly amused at my horrified expression. "By me."

Oh my goodness. I cover my face, groaning out loud because this is the Liam I know, the Liam who loved to drive me crazy.

"Come on, let's go get you fed." He pries my hands from my face, laughing at me. I glare at him for daring to laugh at me, and he tugs on my hand and leads me to the entrance of the burger joint.

"What do you want to eat?" he asks, pushing me into a booth. I smack his hands off of me, and he just chuckles.

How rude.

He sits down beside me, and a waitress plops down two menus in front of us. "You know there is a whole booth directly in front of me?" I point at the seat.

"So."

So? "So why didn't you sit there?"

He gives me a sideways glance, looking at his menu.

"Liam?" I poke his side.

He grunts, twisting away from me but otherwise ignoring me.

"Liaaaaam."

He finally looks at me, completely amused. "Maybe I just wanted to sit next to you."

Well, that shuts me up. I suck my lips into my mouth trying to stop my smile. I look down at the menu, but I already know what I am getting because I get the same thing every time I am here.

"What can I get you guys?" the waitress asks us. I order a huge burger, and Liam orders two of them.

I take out my phone, pointedly trying to ignore him.

He laughs and settles down in the seat, moving closer to me, of course. "Are you trying to ignore me?" He pokes my side.

When we were teenagers we made it our mission to aggravate each other. He did everything to ruffle my feathers, and I retaliated. I hum to myself, gnawing on my bottom lip, trying to stop myself from laughing or smiling. He chuckles and his hand settles on the back of my neck, his finger twining around my hair. He smirks and tugs on my hair, and I knock his hand away. I lean farther away from him, pressing my back against the wall. My stomach growls for the tenth time. I rub my stomach, and his eyes follow my movements.

"Hungry?" he asks. I nod, leaning my head against the booth. I am utterly exhausted, and I know a huge part of the problem is that I haven't eaten in over twelve hours. "I haven't eaten since breakfast."

He huffs loudly then gives me an angry look. "You need to take care of yourself."

"I was too busy taking care of others," I point out.

He shakes his head. "You can take care of others, but don't forget about yourself. You have low blood sugar, remember?"

He remembered. When I was seventeen I felt tired and weak all the time. He demanded that I go to the doctor, and I found out that I have low blood sugar. It's totally under control as long as I eat.

I take my hair tie off my wrist and throw my hair up in a bun at the top of my head. "Well, I have not had issues with it in a long time."

He grunts and looks around the room; I can tell that he has not let his guard down. His body is taut, ready for anything. It really makes me wonder what has gone down with the MC. I was warned that something was happening.

I wish that none of this was going down, especially since he just got home. He needs a break and to relax because I cannot even fathom what went on over there.

Every time I've seen him over the years, he's seemed harder, darker—the things he's seen have changed him. He's definitely a man now. But, right now, he is still my Liam.

A few minutes later the waitress brings our food, setting it down in front of us. I immediately dig in, almost inhaling the whole thing.

I lean back holding my stomach, my eyes closed.

"You sleepy, Paisley?" He nudges my shoulder.

I nod and settle my head on his shoulder.

"You okay to drive home?" he asks, his hand running down my arm, trying to keep me awake.

"Oh yeah, I will be fine." I yawn, sitting up.

"Let me go pay." He slides out of the booth and approaches the front counter. The door to Pat's Burgers opens, and I see three guys. The very same three guys who constantly tried to pick fights with Liam and me. I usually ended up getting the short end of the stick, because I was the easiest one to mess with. Liam was one guy you didn't want to fuck with.

These very guys wanted to be prospects, like Liam, but they are mean and have no loyalty, so the club turned them down flat. Since then, they've made it their life's mission to make my life hell. I was a princess of the Devil Souls, so I had a target on my back. They usually leave Liam alone, but he does not like me being messed with.

I have avoided these guys like a plague. When I see one of them, I run in the other direction or duck behind something to hide.

I duck my head, sliding down in my seat. Hopefully, I can walk to Liam and we can both sneak out without being seen. I don't like trouble; I don't see the point in pettiness that can be avoided altogether. I am by myself a lot. I've been to parties but it's not my scene. In college, I usually stayed in and studied, then went to work.

I've never even been on a date; I just had a lot of girls' nights. I stuck to my promise to wait for Liam.

Now he is home.

"Well, if it isn't Paisley," Tony says.

I slide out of the booth and stand up, facing them. Tony is the one standing in the middle. He has let himself go downhill badly. He has gained a lot of weight, his hair and beard are patchy, and his teeth are yellow and just plain nasty. He has this awful odor; I can barely stand to get within breathing distance of him. I smell the same odor on the other two guys, Billy and James. Very original names.

I plant my hands on my hips. "Tony," I say simply. I am already done with these losers, and only one of them has spoken to me.

"You're looking very nice. The years have done you very good." In unison all three of them look me up and down. Vomit crawls up my throat, and I take a step back. I feel very uncomfortable. Then all three of their heads snap up to look at something behind me. I peek over my shoulder, and I see Liam—and he is pissed off. He splits the distance between us and stands in front of me, his left arm in front of my body.

Protecting me.

The three aggressors look at him like they cannot believe what they are seeing. Tony opens his mouth and closes it while he takes a step back. "Liam, I didn't know you was back, you home for good, man?"

"You have five fucking seconds to leave before I wipe the floor with your faces." Liam's voice is full of rage, his body radiating anger. They turn around and run out of the restaurant like their asses are on fire.

Liam looks at me. "Have they bothered you over the years?" he asks calmly, but I can tell he is anything but that.

I shake my head. "No, I have avoided them."

He relaxes slightly and puts his hand on the small of my back. "You ready to go home?"

I grab my phone off the table. "Yes."

He leads me out of the burger joint, and the three guys are standing outside their trucks. When they spot Liam, they jump inside.

I laugh at their reactions. "I think you made them almost piss their pants."

Liam chuckles and opens my car door. "Pussies, all of them fucking pussies."

I put my phone down in the passenger seat, and Liam pulls out my seatbelt. "Put this on." I click the belt into place. Liam steps away and climbs on his bike; then I am heading home.

Oh boy.

When I arrive home a few minutes later, I step inside the house with Liam right behind me. He's carrying a sack that he took out of his saddle bags. I just bought this house about a month or so ago. It's a large house and it's gated in. All of the women in the club get a salary. It's not as large as the guys' salaries, because they run everything and we don't have to work if we don't want to. I generally love being a nurse.

"Want to rent a movie?" I ask Liam, trying to be calm and chill, though that's not how I feel. I am alone with him, completely and utterly alone with him for the first time since before he left. He studies me, like he can see my nervousness.

"Anything you want," he says.

I let out a deep breath and throw my keys on the shelf by the door. "I am going to go change, pick any guest room you want."

Liam

She is nervous, I can see it written all over her. She hurries into her bedroom, and I spot a bedroom right beside it so I throw my bag on the bed. She left her door cracked slightly, and I see her walking through her room in a pair of black lacy fucking panties.

Fuck me.

Turn the fuck around, Liam, don't lose control right now and throw her across her bed. Her fully clothed is a pain but seeing her in her panties?

Fucking cruel.

I clench my hands, grit my teeth, and walk to the living room, and I sit down on the couch. A few minutes later, she walks out in a pair of sweats and a baggy shirt.

I grin at the shirt because it's the very shirt that she stole from me eight years ago. She stole a lot of my clothes.

"Nice shirt," I tease her and her eyes widen in surprise. She looks down and blushes deeply.

She sits down beside me. I take the blanket off the back of the couch and cover her.

"You remember such small details." She smiles at me sweetly.

I remember everything about her, everything. I have been fucking obsessed since I was seventeen years old, and looking at her now? That's not going to change.

Over the years I would come home and almost fall on my ass every single time I saw her. She has changed over the years, and just when I think she couldn't get more beautiful, I am shocked all over again.

She turns on the TV and lies on my shoulder, her arm wrapping around mine. "Tell me what is happening."

I don't even want her to know this shit, but it affects her so she has to know. I don't want this shit to touch her.

"A cartel has moved in on the Grim Sinners' town, but we got information that they are here too." I am not letting her know that I tortured this information out of them. "They want our towns, to take them over and use us to pump their drugs through the entire US. They planned to get rid of us in any way necessary, and that means attacking us where it fucking hurts."

She freezes; I can tell she is thinking about my words. She sits up and looks at me. "They are gunning for the women and kids." Her voice is barely above a whisper. I can see the fear in her eyes, the tremble of her lips.

I wrap my hand around the side of her neck and face. "They will not fucking touch you," I tell her, looking her straight in the eye. They will not fucking touch her; I will fight everyone on this planet to make sure that doesn't happen. The cartel just made the worst fucking mistake of their lives.

One that is deadly.

Paisley

I pretend to be asleep. Liam is stroking the sides of my face, his thumb stroking my cheekbone. He slides to the end of the couch, his movements gentle. He wraps one arm around my back and slides the other under my knees, lifting me off the couch.

Butterflies swarm my stomach. I can feel the strength and power radiating off of him as he carries me.

He settles me down on the bed, pulling the blanket up under my neck. Fingers push my hair out of my face, and warm lips touch my forehead. I almost jump out of my skin, but I hold strong.

"Good night, my love," he whispers softly.

A few minutes later the door is shut with a soft click. I open my eyes, press my hand over my heart and stomach, and bury my head into the pillow, giggling.

Liam

I can hear her giggling through the door, and I grin. Check-fucking-mate.

two

Paisley

I wake up to the smell of coffee and bacon. Who is in my house? I look at the ceiling, thinking back to yesterday.

Liam.

He is home and in my house. He is home for good. I slide out of bed and walk into the kitchen.

I stop instantly once I see him. Dear God, give me strength. He is shirtless, tattoos running up and down his body, the muscles in his back flexing while he plates the food.

He turns around and looks at me, and my breath catches in my throat at the sight of his eight pack. Are those even legal? He clears his throat, and I tear my eyes away from his abs. His eyebrow arches and he smirks. Busted. I look at everything in the room but him. My face burns with embarrassment.

"What do you want to drink?" I can't help but notice the amusement in his voice.

Fuck me.

"Water is good."

He takes out two bottles of water, puts them under his arm, and picks up both plates.

"You made me breakfast."

He is a sweetheart. He has always been a sweetheart. He's always gone out of his way for people, doing things that others wouldn't think about doing. I walk ahead of him into the living room and plop down on the couch, and he sits directly beside me. He hands me a plate of eggs, bacon, and toast.

"Thank you." I smile and dig into my food. I am a foodie. I love any and all food, and I eat a lot of it. Thank goodness I have a high metabolism, or I would be screwed.

"You have work today?"

"Yeah," I grumble. Any other day I would be happy to leave for work, but not today because I want to spend the day with him.

"What time do you have to be in?" he asks.

"Four."

He nods. "You mind dropping me off at the clubhouse so I can get my truck? Then I will follow you to work."

"Okay, that works for me." I shrug.

We arrive at the clubhouse around three o'clock, and my father is the first person to step outside. He looks at me and then at Liam, who his keeping me by his side.

"Hey, baby girl." Dad pulls me away from Liam, who snatches the back of my pants, not allowing me to go far. Dad glares at him, and Liam stares right back. The pissing match is for real with these two, and it's only gotten worse. Neither would admit it, but they secretly like each other.

I roll my eyes at the two of them, and I spot my stepmother, Kayla, standing at the entrance looking highly amused. I pull away from them and they reluctantly let go.

Kayla pulls me into a hug. "I can't believe he has gotten this hot," she whispers into my ear and I laugh. She is right, he is a man now. All man. He is not what you would call pretty; he is huge and muscular and looks like a badass. He is beautiful, in his own way.

A way that I love.

"Tell me about it," I whisper back. She giggles and Dad turns around to eye her. "Busted." I laugh. She ducks into the warehouse, pulling me with her.

I spot my little brother playing with the other little kids, and he looks up and sees me. My heart lightens at the sight of his beautiful smile. He is now ten years old, and it's so hard to believe.

He walks over to me and hugs me.

"Hey, little bro." I muss up his hair, and he ducks and gives me the look. The look that is my father's, the very one that tells me I am in deep shit. This never fazed me as a kid. I knew that I had him wrapped around my little finger. I learned, from a young age, that I just had to act all sad and cute and I'd get my way. If Dad said no, I would just go to one of the other guys in the club. It was great being the only girl for so long.

Butcher walks into the room and sees me. He waves me over and I hug his middle. Then I hug Techy and Kyle. I haven't seen them in a couple of weeks; work has been getting the best of me.

"How is work?" Kyle asks, leaning against the table.

I grin. "I love it, but it's tiring. Seems to be a lot of gunshot wounds here lately." I look at them pointedly.

They tense and look at each other. I guess they had something to do with that. The door opens and in walks

Liam

Liam. He spots me and walks over, and he shakes hands with Butcher, Techy, and Kyle.

"Good to have you home, Liam," Kyle tells him.

Liam looks at me and then back at them. "Good to be fucking home."

I hide my smile and look at Kayla, who is practically swooning over Liam. Dad is just glaring at him like he is the cause of all his troubles.

Liam

Her father is pissed at me, but I couldn't give two fucks. The moment the door to the warehouse shut, with Paisley inside, he threatened me to keep me away from her.

I told him, and I fucking quote, "She is mine and you will have to kill me before I'll leave her." That's why he is pissed, and I don't blame him. I will be the same if I am lucky enough to have a daughter someday, and I honestly hope that I don't. Too many fuckers in this world. I have firsthand knowledge of how horrible people can be.

"Bye you guys, love you." She waves and I follow her out of the clubhouse. I can feel the eyes glaring at my back. I flip them off and they all laugh. I couldn't give two fucks what they think. We all know that Paisley and me is something that is going to happen.

Paisley

Liam walks me to the hospital entrance. My stomach is in knots because I am not sure what I need to do or say. We are in a weird place where I don't know what is going on. I thumb the strap of my bag, gnawing on my bottom lip. "I

31

guess I will head on in," I tell him, and he takes a step closer.

I hold my breath waiting to see what he will do. His face bends down, his lips settling on my forehead. "Have a good day at work, Baby." I close my eyes, enjoying feeling him against me.

"You have a nice day too," I tell him and he lets me go. I turn around and put my hand over my mouth, trying to seem calm and collected, when I am anything but that.

Vanessa looks at me, wide eyed. "Girl, he has it bad." She groans. "I am so jealous!" She screeches the last part.

I laugh and put my back on my locker. She eyes me up and down. "You've had this man hooked since he was seventeen years old. You're a goddess."

I laugh again. "He has had me hooked too. The moment I laid eyes on him, I was a goner."

She nods.

There is a knock on the door and it's pushed open, revealing an amused Liam. I'm probably as pale as Vanessa is right now. "Want me to bring you lunch?" he asks, his eyes full of laughter.

Oh my god, did he hear what I just said? My heart feels like it just skipped a beat. "I will text you when I am going on break," I manage to get out.

"Alright." He winks and starts to shut the door; then he peeks in again.

I gulp.

"I am a goner for you too, Baby."

My mouth opens and I stare at the now-closed door, then at Vanessa, who is sitting on the booth clutching her chest.

"Oh my god," I whisper over and over while I try to wrap my head around what just happened.

Vanessa manages to laugh. "You're so fucked," she says gleefully.

I can't believe he just said that. One thing I know for certain; you couldn't take the smile off my face even if you tried.

A Few Hours Later

Today has sucked, completely and utterly. It isn't even lunchtime yet and it sucks, because guess who broke their arm?

Tony!

The very same guy who was starting to harass me at Pat's—until he saw Liam, that is—and to top it all? I was assigned to be his nurse.

Life is just perfect, isn't it?

Now I have to walk in there and give him some pain medications. I let out a deep breath and plaster on a fake smile as I step into the room.

Tony sits up in bed, grinning. "Well, if I knew you was going to be my nurse, I would have broken my arm sooner." His grin is creepy, sending chills up my back.

"I am here to give you pain meds." I give him the shot. "You should feel better soon." I can feel his eyes burning into me, and I just want to get out of here. This guy makes me feel totally uncomfortable just by being in my presence. I turn around, avoiding looking at him.

A hand wraps around one of my ass cheeks, pinching. I gasp and whirl around, my fist landing on his cheekbone. "Do not ever fucking touch me!" I yell into his face and he laughs. His uninjured hand grabs his dick, and his tongue shoots out, licking his bottom lip.

I am shaking with anger. I hate him. I walk out of the room, and I hear Vanessa call my name. I step into the locker room, trying to contain myself so I don't walk in there and beat the shit out of him.

The door opens behind me. "Vanessa, I am fine," I tell her without looking around, not wanting her to see my angry tears.

"Why the fuck wouldn't you be fine?" Liam asks.

Well, of course it would be him. I count to ten and look around. Liam looks me over, and he sees my tears. He sets my food down on the chair and stalks over to me, his face like stone.

"Who bothered you?"

I shake my head. "Liam..." I start to argue, not wanting trouble. He interrupts me, his hand pressed to the back of my neck. "Who. The. Fuck. Bothered. You."

"Tony," I whisper.

Liam searches my face, shaking with anger, his jaw clenching and unclenching. "What did he do?"

I duck my head. I don't want him to know.

"What the fuck did he do!" he yells and I close my eyes. I finally tell him, "He grabbed my ass."

"He did what?" He lets me go and pushes me gently into the seat. "Eat your food, Baby," he says gently and he walks out of the room. I stare at the door.

What is he going to do?

I open my bag to see he brought me Mexican food. I know, in moments like these, there is absolutely no way to stop him or any of the other guys from doing what they want. If I weren't worried about getting fired, I would have drug that fucker out by his hair myself.

Not even five minutes later, Liam walks back in the room and kisses the top of my head. "Have a nice rest of the day." He winks and then he is gone.

I guess it went well?

I hurry and finish my food, and I walk to Tony's room. I see a doctor examining his other arm, Vanessa looks at me. "It seems that he fell getting out of bed and broke his other arm."

I cover my mouth to stop my laughter, my stomach aching from holding it in. I duck into the bathroom, not able to restrain myself any longer.

I am finally off work. I get a text from Liam letting me know that he is at the entrance waiting on me. I look through the glass door to see him standing there.

"Well, it seems someone fell and broke their other arm," I tease and he shrugs.

"I knew he was a clumsy fucker, with that ugly mug. It could do with some decorating."

"Yeah, yeah." I wave my hand. He walks me over to my car and helps me inside, looking around the parking lot.

"Anything new happen?" I ask.

He shakes his head. I shut my door and he climbs on his bike. Tomorrow is my day off, and I am ready to sleep in and relax.

I get to the house a few minutes later, and the gate slams shut behind me. Using my phone, I alarm the high-tech gate and fence Techy installed around my house.

"If Tony pulls shit like that again, I won't be as nice," Liam warns me, his hand pressed to my back.

"Well, if you call breaking his arm *nice*," I tease and unlock my door before stepping inside.

Liam's expression darkens. "Nobody fucks with you, Paisley. That shit won't happen."

He is after my heart.

"You off work tomorrow?" he asks.

"Yes."

That slow, sexy smile takes over his face. "Tomorrow, I am taking your ass out on a date." He goes into his room as I gape at his back.

I guess that means I have a date with Liam. This will be our first date and I am thrilled, but I've got to admit that this is new territory and I am bit nervous.

You would think I wouldn't be because I have known him for so long. We have been friends or in the in-between place since we were teenagers. But that is not the case. This is different. This is the beginning of what he said all those years ago, and I quote:

"I am coming for you, Paisley."

Oh boy.

Liam

I look at her standing in the kitchen, staring at the wall, speechless. I grin and go into my room, mission number one accomplished.

Check-fucking-mate.

three

Paisley

Breathe, I tell myself while I put the finishing touches on my makeup and hair. Liam is waiting in the living room while I am getting ready.

Liam has hung around the house mowing my lawn, binge-watching TV, and just doing whatever. I slept almost all day long; I needed to catch up on sleep.

But now, we are going on our first date, and I am nervous--beyond nervous. This is my first date ever. Liam was my first and only kiss, mind you. At twenty-six years old, I am as innocent and virginal as they get.

Which is almost pathetic if you think about it.

I unplug my straightener from the wall and put away my makeup. I take a step back, admiring myself. I am wearing white skinny jeans and black boot-leg heels. My top is black lace, and the sleeves are open to mid-shoulder.

You got this! I encourage myself and open the bathroom door, walking straight to the living room without thinking.

Liam stands when he sees me enter and his mouth opens, and I smirk. His eyes narrow on my mouth before his eyes move up and down, raking over my body.

"Fucking beautiful."

I couldn't stop my enormous grin even if I wanted to. "Well, thanks." I wink, spinning around slowly so he can get the full effect. My butt looks fabulous in these pants.

"Don't do that shit." He grabs my hand to stop me, and I snort trying to control my laughter.

His eyes narrow on me. "Let's go, we have reservations," he says grumpily, and I grin at the back of his head as he pulls me along.

Liam

She knows exactly what she fucking does to me. She has an amazing ass, which she catches me staring at quite often. She spun around, letting me get a full view.

Fuck me, doesn't she look beautiful?

It's pure torture, plain and fucking simple. She knows what she does to me, and she likes to tease me. It's fucking torture.

She keeps looking out the window trying to hide her smile, but I see that shit. I held out for years because we wanted to wait until I was out of the SEALs before working on a relationship. But now I am out of the SEALs, and all bets are off. And waiting is becoming more and more painful.

Being a SEAL is something you have to be determined to do, because it will forever change you. The shit I saw over there is tough. I had friends die, and some were captured. Tortured. That kind of shit will never leave you.

Over the years I learned that I will never deserve someone like Paisley, but now I don't give a fuck. I am going to be selfish and I am going to have her anyway.

"What has you thinking so hard?"

Paisley

Liam is staring out the windshield intensely. "What has you thinking so hard?" I ask.

He tilts his head toward me, a smile tugging at his lips. "You."

I arch an eyebrow, my stomach knotting. "Me?"

He lifts my hand to his mouth, where he presses a gentle kiss. I shiver. "Yes, you." He smirks.

"You're sweet." My stomach is in knots.

I love this side of him. He is smiling sweetly at me, which is something I rarely see from him. He looks at me fully. "Only to you."

My heart. I am not sure I can take sweet Liam right now. I hide my face, trying to hold back the smile and not look like a loon.

We pull up in front of the nicest restaurant in town. Liam opens my door and lifts me from the truck.

Liam doesn't have a beard like most of the other guys. He is clean-shaven, but he has a rugged look that is just all man.

"I am starving," I tell him, and my stomach growls for the tenth time since we left. I am surprised he hasn't heard it.

He laughs. "I know." He looks pointedly at my stomach.

My mouth opens in shock, and I smack his chest lightly, pretending to be mad. He laughs harder, tugging me into his side for a small hug, which has me smiling like a loon once again. He doesn't let me go. His arm is still wrapped around me, pressing me against his side, as we walk inside the restaurant. He gives his name and we are soon seated.

I fully expect him to sit in front of me, but he picks up his chair and sits beside me once again. I like it. It's different from what a lot of guys do. Honestly, it makes me feel protected. I also feel like he wants me to be close to him—but most of all I feel protected.

Just being in his presence gives me a sense of security I haven't had since I was sixteen. He just has this presence about him.

"You know this feels strange," I confess to him.

His brow furrows in confusion. "What do you mean?"

"This is our first date," I whisper, looking at the restaurant around us.

He kisses my temple. "Fucking adorable." He opens his menu.

I pinch the side of his leg. "I am not adorable."

He laughs and gives me a look telling me I am being ridiculous. "Baby, you're beautiful and you fucking know it."

I smile, ducking my head to look at the menu. I am someone who is pretty confident in who she is because it was ingrained in me. Dad told me to accept who I was and be comfortable with who I was.

So I am.

Liam's hand rubs my back gently. Even though he is not saying anything, it's his way of letting me know he is present. It's the little things like this I notice the most. Even from across the room, he will look at me, make eye contact, and go back to his conversation. In high school he would lock eyes with me, making sure I was okay, and then he would go back to his class.

High school was, honestly, a rough time for me because everyone knew what went down with the school janitor. Many of the girls went around saying I attacked him.

Liam

A lot of the guys were even worse because they thought it was my fault. They had the idea in their heads that I was easy. These guys included Tony and his friends.

Liam was my safe haven.

He even stayed back a grade so he would be with me until I was out of high school, which is why he was nineteen when he left.

"What has you thinking so hard?" he asks.

I look at him. "I was thinking of high school and everything you did for me."

"Those fuckers need their asses beat." He smirks. "Again."

I laugh because Liam did get into a lot of fights. "I don't know how you didn't get kicked out, honestly."

"The MC," he confesses.

"Of course it was." I laugh again. I knew the MC played a huge part in it because Liam was standing up for me, plus he was a prospect.

"Are you happy to be home, Liam?" It's something I've been dying to ask since the moment he got home.

With me.

His eyes search my face, and I can tell he is catching my double meaning. I internally wince, awaiting his answer. He touches the side of my face. "I am more than happy being home, Baby."

Swooning is the word you could use to describe me right now. I wink. "Well, I guess I am sort of happy to see you home," I tease.

He chuckles before digging his fingers into my side, causing me to laugh loudly, way too loudly for this type of restaurant. I cover my mouth while attempting to push him away. The waitress comes back, frowning, but she gives us a break. She smiles at both of us after she gets our drink

41

order. "How long have you guys been together? You are a beautiful couple."

I start to tell her that we aren't together, but Liam beats me to the punch. "Ten years."

Oh my god, he is trying to steal my heart, isn't he? She presses her order pad to her chest. "Oh my goodness, that is so cute!" She sighs, looking at both of us. "I will put your drink orders in."

I have no clue what to say to Liam. He is shaking with silent laughter. He did this shit on purpose to leave me speechless. "Mean ass," I whisper loudly.

He bursts out laughing, holding his stomach, and I shove a piece of bread into his mouth to shut him up.

He pulls the bread from his mouth and goes back to laughing. So I do the only thing a sensible adult can do: I pout, folding my arms across my chest.

He instantly catches on to what I am doing and pulls me into his lap. Which instantly changes my pouting to internally freaking out.

I am in Liam's lap, holy crap.

I lick my lips, staring wide eyed at Liam, whose eyes are full of desire. "Oh boy," I whisper out loud. Liam's head gets closer and closer to me, his mouth stopping at my ear. "Not here."

I slide out of his lap, trying to ignore the hard bulge. My mouth is dry, and my face is burning with embarrassment. What do you expect from a girl who is still a virgin at twenty-six years old? Liam is the only guy I have kissed, and no one has touched me down there besides me.

The waiter returns with our drinks, and I thank her. After I order, I'm silent. What do I say?

"Fuck," Liam says. I follow his gaze to see my former best friends, who abandoned me to make my life hell.

"Just ignore those bitches." I turn away from them and he nods, trying to hide his smile. He scoots his hand under the table, twining our fingers together.

I lean over and lay my head on his shoulder, trying to stop my rising anxiety at the thought of being in the same room as these people. It should not affect me, but these people made my life hell. There is stuff that Liam does not know about. They would try to jump me in the girls' bathroom and the locker room, and they'd trip me and hurt me any way they possibly could.

It was hell. I am a person who will take up for herself, but it will destroy you living on the edge twenty-four and seven. I don't want anything to ruin this moment; I want to have the perfect first date with Liam. Wishful thinking, isn't it?

Paisley

Wishful thinking it was. Liam and I had an amazing dinner. They stayed away, and we spent the whole time getting to know each other better and having fun, enjoying being in each other's company.

Liam and I walk hand-in-hand out of the restaurant to see six people waiting for us.

Why me?

Liam tightens his grip on me, staring at the wall of people: Holly, Janice, and Beatrice, my three ex-best friends from high school, and their husbands. I have not seen them since I got home from college years ago. Time hasn't done these three girls any favors. They let themselves go. If they were in the restaurant at all, I guarantee they ate and ran off without paying or used someone else's credit card.

"Well, if it's isn't Paisley!" Janice's hands rest on her hips. She is wearing a belly shirt with a pair of shorts so short that I think they were meant to be underwear.

"What do you want?" I ask her in a bored voice. I want nothing to do with this. This is beyond ridiculous, and I just had an amazing night.

All three of the girls are staring at Liam. I think in high school they were mad that Liam and I were so close. And now he's back. That could be why they are doing this.

"Look, this should have been left in high school. Let's just go our separate ways and be done with it," I tell her, smiling. Liam lets his hand fall from my back and moves in front of me as if he is ready to push me behind him at a moment's notice.

The three girls laugh at me mockingly, and I know it's not going to end well.

Did I mention that I have taken kickboxing for the past couple of years?

From the corner of my eye, I spot the three men moving closer to Liam. Liam stiffens at my side, so I know he has seen the same thing.

On the other hand, I think I need this. I think it is time for me to get revenge. They hurt me throughout high school. I am not the same girl. If they want to fight, we can.

"Quit hiding behind your man." Beatrice laughs loudly.

Fuck it.

I step out from behind Liam and grab a hair tie off my wrist; then I bend down and take off my heels.

Liam touches my shoulder. "Paisley?"

"Alright who's first?"

All three girls look at me, then at each other, in shock.

"You guys have been itching to do this for fucking years, let's get it over with." My voice is devoid of emotion.

Janice steps forward first and charges toward me. She reaches for my hair first thing. How original. I grab hers, wrenching her head to the side, and bring my fist up, smashing it into her face over and over until it's covered in blood.

I kick my leg out, tripping her, and she hits the ground with a thud. I look up and see Liam's face connecting with another guy's face, knocking him out. He hits the ground next to the other two men.

The other girls scream and run toward me. Liam grabs Beatrice's hair. "You will not fucking jump her," he snarls at her; then he lets her go.

I was so distracted by Liam that I forgot about Holly, and she tackles me to the ground. The wind is knocked out of me, and her hand connects with my face in a bitch slap.

"A bitch slap, really?" I flip her over onto her back and punch her hard in the face twice, making a hard crunching sound.

She reaches up, touching her mouth, and spits out a tooth. I stand up, knowing she is done. I walk over to Beatrice, grip the back of her head, and slam it down on the top of Liam's truck, knocking her out.

"Bitch," I hiss.

Liam is staring at me with his arms across his chest and a shit-eating grin on his face.

"Bitches had it coming."

He laughs and opens the passenger door for me, and I climb inside. The three guys are up at this point and are carrying their women out of there.

"Proud of you, Paisley," Liam says after he shuts his door, and I watch them leave, walking into the dark.

"They tortured me long enough."

His eyes darken, and his jaw clenches. "They fucking did and they won't fuck with you again." His eyes search my face, locking on my mouth.

In a split second, his hand is fisting in my hair and his mouth is pressed firmly against mine. I gasp in shock, and he takes that second while my mouth is wide open to fully kiss me.

His hand rests on my cheek, his lips moving over mine in a way I can't describe, and my body is reacting to it. My hand slides down his chest and under his shirt. I have been wanting to touch his abs for years. I sigh, sinking harder into him, and his fingers pull on my hair, tilting my head back even further. He growls and bites my bottom lip. I groan and move closer.

This goes on a couple of minutes, my hands moving all over his body. A car door slams next to ours and I pull back, my head falling to his shoulder.

"I have been wanting to do that for a long time," I confess and he chuckles huskily. I sit back in my seat and buckle my seatbelt.

He starts the truck and we head home.

four

A Few Hours Later

Paisley

I take a long shower to wash off the dirt from the fight; then I walk into the living room. I am having a hard time wrapping my brain around the thought that I got into a fight with three girls tonight, the three girls who tortured me throughout high school. I hadn't seen them for years.

Until tonight.

Liam is leaning back in the recliner watching TV. He looks up when I walk into the room. He studies me. I am wearing another one of his shirts, which I stole right from his suitcase, and a pair of baggy sweats.

I am nervous and, honestly, slightly ashamed of myself for fighting, because that is not me, but I felt like it needed to be done. I had a deep sinking feeling their shit was going to start because Liam is back.

Liam pats his lap, and I stare at the very lap he just patted. He wants me to sit there? I suck my bottom lip between my teeth thinking, *what should I do?*

That last time I was in his lap an erection was under me.

His eyes narrow and he curls his finger, motioning for me to come over. Throwing caution to the wind, I walk to him. He smirks and, leaning forward, he grabs my hips and sets me right in his lap.

"Now was that so hard?"

My mind goes back to the restaurant—his dick. *Yeah, you don't want me answering that.* "Yeah, it was." I sigh, like it was the hardest thing in the world for me to do.

He leans farther back in the seat, pulling me along with him. My head rests under his chin. "I missed you, Liam." Moments like these make me think.

His hand runs up my arm, to my shoulder blade, to my neck, causing me to shiver. "I missed you too, Baby." His voice is so deep. God, his voice has only gotten deeper over the years. It's deep, rusty, and just absolutely amazing—it sends shivers down my spine.

Tonight was our first date, and that part of the night was absolutely amazing. Those girls came along and tried to ruin it, and Liam stopped one of them from jumping me.

I snort loudly, and he jolts under me. "What's funny?" he grumbles in that voice. Goodness me.

"You grabbed her by her hair." I laugh, remembering the sight of her face when he told her not to jump me.

He chuckles, going back to running his hand over my arms and shoulders. "That shit doesn't fly with me."

Smirking, I say confidently, "I probably could have taken her."

He laughs loudly, his head thrown back. I smack his chest lightly. "What? You think I couldn't?" I sit back, looking at him.

He looks serious, his hand coming up to cup the side of my face. "Sure you could, Baby, you're a badass."

He is totally mocking me. "You better not be—" I don't finish. His lips are on mine once again. My eyes shut. I don't think I will ever get used to the feeling of his lips.

One hand is curled around my face, controlling my movements. His lips move over mine, like he is making love to them. Pulling, sucking, and licking. His other hand is stroking my back tenderly under my shirt. I shift myself in his lap until I am straddling him. I just want to get closer.

My hand sinks into his hair and, as he sits up, my back arches. His dick is growing harder and harder under me. It's literally taking everything in me not to grind myself against him.

He grabs my ass, and I jolt and accidentally press myself hard against him. I can feel my face turning hot with embarrassment.

He stops kissing me, his eyes on my face. Oh my god, he can see me blushing. He smiles sweetly—he can tell, for sure. "Paisley, Baby, never be embarrassed. If it was up to me, I would be making you come over and over. You're not ready for that, yet."

He is right. We may have been friends for a while, but we haven't explored this part of us yet—this is new territory.

My face is still burning with embarrassment as he moves toward me, and my eyes close, thinking he is about to kiss me, but instead he starts kissing my entire face. I laugh, trying to push him away, but he continues kissing me everywhere, and his fingers dig into my sides.

"Mercy!" I scream, tears rolling down my face from laughing so hard.

He finally relents, a beautiful full smile on his face. "You're so beautiful." He pulls me into a hug.

Is he not the sweetest man alive?

God must really love me—or I must have done something that he is proud of—to have blessed me with such a man.

My mind wanders to the thought of sleeping in his arms all night long, something I have often fantasized about.

"Want to cuddle with me? Sleep in my bed tonight?" My words come out in a rush, before my brain can catch on.

He never says a word, but stands up with me in his arms. I guess that he is for it. He pulls back the blanket and sets me down on the sheet.

He settles down beside me, grabbing the remote off the nightstand, and turns on the TV. It lights the room with a soft glow. I scoot over in the bed, making more room, and he lies down beside me. I take my cue and lay my head on his hard, muscular chest.

Liam

I look down at her, lying on my chest, her hair fanned out behind her. She is beautiful; it's hard to believe that I am with her right now.

I have wanted her for ten long fucking years and, a couple of times during my years as a SEAL, I thought I might never come home. The thought of her, home, and the prospect of us being together someday kept me going.

Tonight those three fucking bitches reared their heads once more. They made her life hell throughout high school. They were her friends until the moment the janitor attacked her, and then everything changed.

They did shit that I never knew about until years later. Paisley held on to the fact that they were her friends at one point in time. She isn't a violent person; she'd rather talk through shit. But tonight, she did exactly what she needed to do and beat the shit out of them.

I am not that fucking way. I'd rather knock you the fuck out than deal with your shit. I have always had this overwhelming need to protect her from the world, to protect her sweetness. She has been a huge part of me since she was sixteen and staring at me with her big eyes.

A hand pats my face. "Go to sleep, Liam," she whispers, dropping her hand and snuggling in deeper.

I smile into the dark room. This is what I have waited so many fucking years for.

My Paisley.

Paisley

I stare at the entrance to the hospital in dismay. I want to be anywhere but here. I want to spend every minute with Liam I possibly can.

"What's wrong?" he asks, but I continue staring at the hospital.

"I don't want to work today." I cross my arms across my chest, pouting.

He laughs, his hand wrapping around my throat gently and pulling me over, and he kisses the side of my face. "I will be waiting for you here, when you're off."

I smile. "That will be the highlight of my day."

His eyes darken, his hand tightening on me. "Fuck yeah, it is." He splits the distance between us and kisses me with a deep, raw passion that makes my toes curl.

I pull away, biting my bottom lip. "My day is already better." I wink and step out of the car.

"Paisley, what did I say about that shit?"

I laugh and wait for him to walk around the truck. He grabs my hand and walks me to the front door. It's only a few feet away, but Liam is extremely protective. He has been that way since we were teenagers. But now? He is on another playing field.

We walk inside the door, and he leans down and kisses me one last time. My fingers twist into his shirt as I kiss him back hard.

I break free, kiss his cheek, and reluctantly let him go., His hand is firmly planted on my ass. I blush, stepping back.

"Bye, Baby," he says and I walk through the door, waving at him.

Liam

I've gotten a text from Kyle every hour telling me to come meet the new prospects, who have been going through the process for six months already. It's not easy becoming a full-fledged member. It takes a full two years of experience to even be considered. They want my opinion on these guys, and that's why I am here.

The five prospects stand up as I walk into the club. Respect, check one. I look all of them over. I can tell three of them are military and the other two are not. I like the three military guys instantly. "Military?" I ask them, since they are in the front. The other two guys are already sitting down, looking almost fucking bored.

"Marines, my name is Shane." He shakes my hand, looking me dead in the eye. Check number fucking two.

The other guy stands up. "Marines also, Brett."

Now the last guy. I finally get a good fucking look at him. "No fucking way. Tyler?" He laughs and hugs me.

We were in basic together, but then we were sent to different bases. "How have you been, man?" I ask and he steps back.

"I just got out a year ago. I remember you talking about the MC and decided why not give it a go? How's Paisley?" he asks, giving me a sly fucking smile.

He knows all about her, probably because I annoyed the shit out of him because she was all I talked about. "Why don't you come over for dinner and you can meet her?"

He nods, raising his beer.

I face the other two guys, and they look me up and down like I am shit beneath their shoes. "I'm Todd and this is Chris."

"I'm Liam. I have been a patch member since I was nineteen years old. Let's fucking sit over here so we can talk and see why you guys think you deserve to be a part of the club."

Tyler smacks me on the back and walks to the table with the other two military guys, Shane and Brett. The guys I do not fucking like swagger over like they own this shit.

I pull out a chair and face all of them, and I look them over. Todd smirks at me. I arch an eyebrow, dying for him to say something so I can beat his ass.

"Being in this club is a fucking brotherhood, once you become a full-fledged member you will have a family that will fight, kill, and die for you. That includes your woman, kids, and anyone you care about."

"I left the SEALs a year ago, and I want that brotherhood back," Tyler says, and the other two nod in agreement. Todd and Chris just look around the room.

"If you manage to fucking get into the club, which I doubt a few of you will..." I eye Todd and Chris. They won't make it another month unless they clean up their shit. "You will be set for life and so will your family. Starting wage is five hundred thousand a year, and that will continue to grow. If something were to happen to you, your family would be forever taken care of. Prospecting into the club is not easy. If you make it a year then good luck to you, because the second year is hell."

Chris's hands smack the table, and I glare at him. "How? Cleaning the toilets?" He throws his head back, laughing.

"After we are fucking done with you, you will be begging to clean toilets." His laughter stops immediately.

Todd rolls his eyes. "Like you had to do shit. You was a fucking teenager when you became a member, and we all know how you got in."

"I got into the club because I busted my ass. I did shit even grown fucking men couldn't do. Don't come to me with this *easy* shit, I had it harder than you ever fucking will." I took on the job and was trained in being a torturer. That is what I am fucking good at, and I learned it at age fucking eighteen. It was what I wanted to learn, and I had to go through intense shit to learn it. It made fucking hell week in the SEALs a walk in the park.

"We all know you got in for saving the princess."

I sit still. Tyler's eyes widen and someone mutters, "Fuck."

"What did you say?"

Todd leans in. "We all know you got in for rescuing Paisley."

Chris laughs. "I bet you're fucking glad to be home, she is one beautiful woman. I have tried for six months to get in with that. She told me to back the fuck off."

Fire is burning me from the inside out. The shit they are spewing from their mouths will have them fucking dead.

Todd leans over the table, facing me. "So how did you do it? Keep a woman as beautiful as that piece of pussy locked down for ten years? I bet it's tight as shit." He moans, his hand reaching down toward his dick.

I throw my head back laughing, and he and his friend fucking laugh right along with me.

This fucking guy is the stupidest motherfucker in the world. Todd looks almost gleeful, and he nudges his friend like he has this shit in the bag.

I stand up, my arms resting on the table, smirking at him. "You know what, Todd?"

He laughs again. "What?"

"You're the dumbest motherfucker in the world."

His face turns pale and he looks down; then he stands up, pushing back his chair. "Run!" I taunt him, sliding out of my chair.

He spins around, running for the door. I take out my gun and aim right at the back of his knee. I pull the trigger, and he hits the ground like a pile of rocks.

He screams, holding his knee. I laugh again at how pathetic he is. I walk over to him, and Tyler follows. I press my foot on Todd's knee.

He screams loudly. "Oh no! I bet that's tight as shit. I'm sorry!" I press my foot down harder.

"Carry him to interrogation room three," I tell Tyler, Shane, and Brett. I look at the other fucker. "Get your ass out of here." Chris runs out of the room without a second glance.

Tyler and Shane lift Todd off the ground and carry him out of the room. I stare at the fucker until he is out of sight.

You can do a lot to me, and I will not care one fucking bit. But you fuck with Paisley, I will fucking kill you and do it laughing. You do not disrespect her. You do not do one single fucking thing to her unless you want to die or be tortured within an inch of your life.

You do not mess with her.

"What the fuck is going on?" Paisley's father, Torch, walks into the room with Kyle and Techy on his ass.

"Replay the tapes, Techy, and show him." I am still pissed off beyond fucking belief.

Techy takes out his phone, and the guys gather around as he replays Todd's voice for them, which doesn't help my fucking anger one bit.

Torch stalks out of the room, straight for interrogation room three. I guess the fucker didn't think that her father was the vice president of the club. I step into the room behind Torch to see his fist landing directly on Todd's face. One by one, everyone gets their hits in, beating the shit out of him.

He deserved every fucking second.

I care about Paisley. She is the sweetest girl I have met in my entire life. Nobody disrespects her. She has been my heart since I was seventeen. She already owned me.

"After you dump the fucker off, come over for dinner at eight?" I ask Tyler, and I give him Paisley's address.

He picks the fucker off the ground and tosses him in the back of his truck. He will live, but he will be hurting for a long-ass time.

I get a text from Paisley telling me she is getting off work an hour early.

Paisley

Finally! I think as I walk out of the hospital and straight to Liam's truck. It's parked right in front, and he is leaning against it.

He is the ideal man.

"Hey." I smile at him, and his hands land on my hips, pulling me into him, and he kisses me deeply. I shiver, standing on the tips of my toes, getting closer.

I love that we can do this now; it has been such a long time in the making. Over the years I have stared at his lips wondering what it would be like to kiss him.

He pulls away and kisses my forehead sweetly. "Tyler, my friend from basic, is coming over for dinner—is that okay?" he asks.

I nod instantly. "That is perfectly okay."

Liam opens his door and helps me inside his truck. As he settles into the driver's seat and puts his hands on the wheel, I notice his knuckles are broken.

"Whose ass did you beat today?" I ask him.

He laughs and looks down at his knuckles. "Nobody important, Paisley."

I fold my arms across my chest, smirking. "Mm-hm," I mumble, giving him shit.

He laughs and rubs my thigh. I feel like fire is shooting up my spine.

I can feel Liam looking at me when he is not looking at the road. My face is burning with embarrassment because I reacted that way from just a touch on my thigh. You have to realize that I am a twenty-six-year-old virgin, and that is something not many women can say. The longer I am around him, the more I think about it and the more anxious I am to get to know Liam in that way.

"So when did you meet up with your basic buddy?" I ask him, ready to get my thoughts out of this realm.

"He is one of the prospects for the Devil Souls."

Ahh yeah, I remember meeting a Tyler who is prospecting for the club. "How crazy that he is a prospect after all of these years."

Liam nods. "He remembered me talking about the club and decided to go for it."

"It's awesome that he remembered all of these years. I am glad you have your friend back."

Liam shakes his head, smirking at me. He pulls the truck to a stop in my driveway.

"What is it?"

"You."

My stomach sinks. What does he mean *me*?

He looks at me finally. "You're just the sweetest, Baby."

"Oh." My heart is doing flips in my chest. My hand rests on my chest, and I can feel it pounding under my palm.

God, my heart may not be able to take it.

Liam

I watch as she sets the dining room table. She is wearing a pair of jeans and my T-shirt, and her hair is hanging in curls down her back.

She is perfect.

I also love the fact that she is wearing my shirt. I don't think that Tyler will try to poach my girlfriend, but that doesn't mean I don't want everyone to know that her ass is mine.

She looks up at me, catching me staring. She smiles and lowers her head, hiding the fact that she is blushing.

It's hard to believe that someone like her has waited for years to be with me. She could have had anyone she ever wanted. But for some unknown reason, she wanted me. One thing I know I won't do is make her regret being with me.

One thing is for certain: fuckers would line up down the block trying to take my place, but that shit is not happening. Todd is lucky to even be breathing; I wanted my bullet to be buried in his head instead of his knee.

I plate the steaks on the grill and walk back inside right as the doorbell rings. Paisley sets the steaks down on the table. "Let your friend in, I got this."

Too fucking sweet.

I open the front door. "Hey man, come in." I hold the door open and he steps inside the house.

Paisley comes around the corner, looking like walking sin. Tyler looks at her and then at me. I know exactly what he is thinking, but the fucker won't say it because I wouldn't like that.

Paisley stands at my side, and I put my hand on her ass. She looks slightly shocked, but she plays it off and reaches out for Tyler. "Nice to meet you, Tyler, I'm Paisley."

He shakes his head. "I heard a lot about you." He gives me a mocking look. "You were all Liam talked about during basic."

She grins at him happily. "I can guarantee my friends all think the exact same thing about me."

Paisley

I bet I could get my friend hooked up with Tyler; he would be perfect for her!

Liam honestly shocked me when he put his hand on my ass. He was staking his claim in front of his friend, and I honestly loved it. I love that he is possessive of me.

What girl wouldn't want that?

Liam sits down beside me at the table, and Tyler is in front of us. Tyler is a good-looking man. He is a big guy, and his hair is slightly longer than Liam's. He has this dangerously tall, dark, and handsome look going on.

"So, Tyler, are you single? I have a friend that is," I blurt out. They would be so cute together.

He and Liam laugh, and Liam runs his hand up and down my leg. I put my hand on top of his, my fingers twining with his.

"Yes, I am." He takes a pull of his beer.

I clap my hands together, wondering how I can get them together. I gasp when it comes to me. "Liam, a blind date!"

He just grins at me, full of amusement. I roll my eyes and look at Tyler, who is chuckling under his breath.

Vanessa seriously needs someone in her life. She needs someone to care about her and make her feel safe. She had a fucked-up childhood, and she's dated but never had a serious boyfriend.

"I will show up," he tells me and I grin at him.

I feel Liam moving closer, and he presses his lips against my ear. "That smile is only meant for me," he whispers. My whole body shivers.

I kiss his cheek. "Alright let's dig in." My stomach growls for the tenth time since I have been home. I am a foodie. I could eat all day long, and then an hour later I would be starving again.

Throughout the meal, Liam is always touching me. He touches my leg or plays with my hair. I love how affectionate he is.

I get out of the shower around ten o'clock, and I slip on another of Liam's shirts and a pair of pajama pants. I walk into my bedroom, only to see Liam lying on his back, shirtless, with his arms behind his head.

God, give me strength not to do unthinkable things right now.

I swallow hard, trying not to let on how affected I am. I throw my clothes in the laundry basket and try to play it cool while walking to the bed, but on the inside I am anything but that.

Liam pulls back the blanket for me, and I slide into bed beside him. I look at him, and he turns over, his thumb pressed into my bottom lip.

"Baby," he whispers, before his mouth brushes mine so softly it's almost feather-like. I dig my fingers into the back of his head. I leave my eyes open, staring deeply into his. I smile, my lips moving against his ever so slightly.

He tilts his head to the side, his thumb stroking my cheek. I giggle, biting my lip, and move my head forward, trying to kiss him.

He lowers his head to kiss the side of my neck. I instinctively tilt my head to the side, his lips nibbling, kissing.

Oh my goodness.

I shiver, lift my leg, and let it rest on the back of his thigh. He takes that cue to move between my legs, still kissing my neck and throat.

His hand slowly slides down my side to my thigh, which is draped over his hip. I want him so much, so much.

He lifts his head, and his eyes are dark with want. His lips finally connect with mine, and I groan and tilt my hips, trying to get any kind of relief. His hand is on my thigh, slowly moving toward...

I freeze, waiting to see what he is going to do.

His hand moves closer and closer, goose bumps trailing in its wake. His finger stops at the edge of my panties, his lips break from mine, and I open my eyes to look at him.

His eyes are searching my face and I nod, giving him the confirmation he is wanting. His fingers wrap around the strap of my underwear, pulling.

I gasp as his thumb presses against my clit. "God," I gasp once again, fire shooting through me.

Liam sits up, removing his hand. He grabs the bottom of my shirt, I lift my arms, and he pulls the shirt over my head and drops it on the floor. He throws my underwear down right along with it, leaving me completely naked under his gaze.

The urge to hide myself is strong. Liam perches himself over me, sliding down my body, his face stopping right above my breast. He looks at me one last time before his mouth latches on.

"Fuck," I hiss, fire shooting straight down to my pussy.

His hand goes back between my legs, his thumb stroking my clit. He switches to the other breast, sucking and pulling.

Driving me insane.

He kisses his way down my stomach, my back arching. My hands are above my head, gripping the headboard.

I can't believe this is happening right now.

His hand leaves, and I look down to see his head right between my legs.

I squeeze my eyes shut—is he really doing what I think he is? I feel his breath right before his tongue drags across my clit. His hands wrap around my thighs, lifting them until they are on his shoulders.

I bring my hands down from above my head to settle at the back of his head. My toes curl, and a finger slowly slides inside me, curling. I throw my head back. My legs are shaking—I am right at the edge.

I clench around his finger, my whole body stiffening. He curls his finger and sucks at the same time, and I come hard.

My whole body is shaking, and I cover my face with my hands, coming down from this amazing orgasm.

Liam kisses both sides of my thigh, and I shiver and look at him. He smooths my hair out of my face, rubbing my cheekbone.

"What about you?" I ask him.

He shakes his head. "Baby, this was about you." He covers me with the blanket, and I turn over and lie on his chest.

"I can't believe that just happened," I whisper and he chuckles loudly. His fingers drift down my back softly. "It will happen again and again, Baby."

Excitement flows through me, butterflies swarming my stomach, and his fingers softly, tenderly rub my back and stroke my hair, causing my eyes to drift closed.

At moments like this it hits me how blessed I am. I have waited for Liam to come home to me since I was eighteen years old, and now I am twenty-six.

The feel of him holding me right now? It was so worth it, and so much more.

"Liam?"

"Yeah, sweet girl?"

I smile into his chest. "I am glad you're finally home."

He kisses the top of my head. "I am glad to be home."

I close my eyes, kiss the back of his hand, and tuck it under my face.

"Goodnight."

"Night, Baby."

five

Paisley

One Week Later

Why did I agree to go fishing with Liam? I regret that decision as I glare at the clock sitting on the nightstand; it reads 4:00 a.m.

He wants to be on the water right at the ass crack of dawn. Don't get me wrong—I love me some fishing—but night fishing is just as great in my opinion.

"Baby." He laughs loudly, pulling at my feet.

I kick my legs, burrowing my head deeper into the pillow and tucking the blanket under my neck.

He laughs again, thoroughly amused by me, apparently. I am not a morning person, not one bit. The blanket under my neck is pulled away, and my hand scrambles trying to catch it.

It's tossed onto the floor, and I look up at Liam, ready to hurt him. He holds his stomach, bent over because he's laughing at me so hard.

"Baby, we have to go! The fish will be biting soon," he informs me, grinning at me ear-to-ear. I am trying to ignore the fact that he is absolutely gorgeous.

"I am cold. I have to brush my hair and get my clothes on," I whine, pulling the shirt I am wearing down over my legs.

He rolls his eyes at me, turns around, and stalks to my closet.

"Did you just roll your eyes at me, Liam?" I ask him, pretending to be mad.

He laughs and comes out of the closet with a pair of jeans, a T-shirt, a jacket, and my muck boots. He puts the stuff on the bed by me, and he grabs the bottom of my shirt, pulling it over my head.

Is he really doing what I think he is right now?

He throws my shirt in the laundry basket by the door; then he bends down and picks my bra up off the ground. He puts the bra on way too easily and grins when I look down in astonishment.

"Baby, I have been tearing that thing off of you for the past week, over and over." He smirks, looking way too pleased with himself.

I blush and cover my face. He is correct; we have been playing and experimenting a lot. I finally went down on him, and I was thoroughly terrified. I had to ask him what to do, and he walked me through it. I was embarrassed because I was so clueless.

He thought it was the cutest thing in the world, of course

Ugh, men. Fuck my life.

Right now he is being the cutest thing alive. He pulls my shirt over my head, and I smile at him. He shakes his head and pulls my jeans over my feet and up to my thighs. Then he wraps an arm around my back, lifts me, and pulls them over my ass, which is a hard feat, mind you, since it's not the smallest thing in the world.

He sets me back down on the bed then walks into the bathroom and comes out with a hairbrush.

"You're the sweetest person on earth."

He glares at me and pulls me to the edge of the bed, and I cross my legs, letting him brush my hair.

"I am not sweet," he grumbles.

I laugh. "Well, you are to me."

The hairbrush stops. "Of course I am, Baby, you're my woman and you deserve to be handed the fucking world."

Be still my heart, I just can't with this person.

"Liam," I choke out, my eyes filled with tears and my throat tight.

The hairbrush stops once more. "You better not be fucking crying, you know what I said about that shit." He tosses the brush on the bed and smacks the side of my ass, drying my tears right up.

"Ouch." I rub the side of my ass.

"Want me to kiss it better?" His eyes darken, looking right at my pussy. I push his chest, getting up. "We both know if you do that we won't go fishing today."

I start to walk past him, and he pulls me close and kisses me hard, his hand landing on my ass once again.

I retaliate. I run my hand up his leg and grab his balls. He jumps and pulls away, looking shocked.

I run into the bathroom, laughing my ass off at the sight of his face.

I laugh at the sight of his face again when I catch another fish. This makes my twentieth fish, and he has gotten three. He is pouting at the front of the boat.

"Aww, Baby, you can have this one," I tell him.

He glares at me and turns around, giving me his back. That isn't a bad view, mind you.

The boat is tied up at a dock. "How about I go on down the water's edge a bit."

He doesn't say a word and I laugh again. I grab my fishing pole and step off the boat. I walk down the stream, still in sight of the boat but far enough away that I won't interfere with Liam.

He nods his approval. The cartel is still a problem, even though they are being quiet lately.

I take out my phone and set my fishing pole down

A little while later, I hear someone walking behind me, and I turn around to see a man carrying the biggest fish. I smile as an idea forms.

"Psst," I say to the man.

He is an older man, probably sixty or so. "Hello, little lady."

"Can I ask you for a favor?"

Liam

"Liam!" Paisley yells, and I look down to see her holding a massive fucking fish.

I don't fucking believe this shit! She's caught every damn fish in this lake today, and now she caught a fish that is almost as big as she is.

I set my fishing pole down and walk off the boat to help her with the fish. Once I reach her, she is grinning ear-to-ear.

Little shit.

"Look!" she says, excited.

"Happy for you, Baby." I grunt. Why the fuck is she catching everything? She laughs loudly, and an old man walks over. Laughing, he takes the fish from her.

She fucking played me.

She laughs harder at the sight of my face, and the old man is almost lying on the ground. I bend down and toss her over my shoulder, and she pinches my ass.

I walk over to the edge of the dock. "Liam, you better—"

She doesn't get to finish what she was trying to say. I toss her into the water, and she pops up, laughing. "I was hot anyway. Thanks, Baby."

Such a little shit.

Paisley

He bends down and holds out his arms. I slip my hands in his, and he pulls me out of the water. I shiver in the colder air; it's just in the seventies today, definitely not swimming weather.

"Fuck." He pulls me hard into his side, walking me toward the boat. He helps me inside and starts pulling clothes and blankets out of the compartments under the seat.

"Change. I will hold the blanket up for you so nobody can fucking see you." He lifts the blanket, but not far enough so he can't watch me change.

I arch an eyebrow, and he smiles and watches me strip out of my clothes. I pull my jeans down, and my phone hits the bottom of the boat.

"You're lucky it's water resistant," I tell him, and I bend down to make sure that it's okay and, luckily, it turns on just fine.

I see a text from Vanessa telling me she is nervous about her date tonight with Tyler. An idea forms, and I smile and delete the text so Liam doesn't see it.

Tonight we are having date night.

I talked Liam into going to dinner with me. We are seated a few booths away from…what do you know! Vanessa and Tyler are on a date tonight.

Liam looks at them and at me, thoroughly amused. "I forgot they were meeting tonight." I shrug while I sneak past Tyler. Vanessa isn't here yet.

Tyler looks up and laughs when he sees us. I hide my face in Liam's chest, trying to control my laughter. Liam pushes me into the booth and settles down beside me.

I notice that he chose the seat facing them; he is nosy too. "You're worried about her."

I look at Liam, nodding. I am worried about her. She doesn't date and, honestly, she is kind of scared of men. She's had a really rough go of it, and I want her to be happy.

"What happened?"

I look at the menu, saddened by thoughts of what she has dealt with in her life. "It's not my story to tell, but she's had a rough go of it. A really bad childhood."

He shakes his head angrily.

"I just want her to be happy. I think Tyler would be perfect for her."

He laughs and kisses the side of my head, and I lay my head against his shoulder. Vanessa walks into the restaurant. I told her his booth number, which is why he got there early.

They still don't know what each other looks like. Vanessa has long dark brown hair that reaches her butt, beautiful brown eyes, and freckles covering her nose and the tops of her cheekbones. She stops staring at the back of Tyler's head, and I can see that she wants to turn around and run back out. She clenches her hands together and walks over to the booth, stopping at the end of the table.

Tyler looks up at her and his mouth falls open, staring at her in awe.

I cover my mouth trying to stop my laughter. Liam presses his lips against my temple, trying to hide his laughter.

Tyler stands up and leans on the table like he can barely stand. He says something and helps her into her seat.

How cute.

I sigh and watch them. I am such a hopeless romantic.

"Come on, Baby, let's sneak out and we can grab some burgers."

I nod. I just wanted to make sure she is okay. We walk out of the restaurant, and I look through the window to see her grinning ear-to-ear. I want her to be happy; she has been my best friend for years.

Tyler is staring at her like she is a freaking goddess and he can't believe she is sitting in front of him right now.

How cute is this!

"Paisley!" someone yells for me.

I turn around to see the very guy who asked me out a month before Liam got home. He works in the hospital as a security guard. Liam wraps his arm around my waist, his grip tight, on edge. I lay my hand on his chest.

The guy walks over, completely ignoring Liam. "How have you been? I haven't seen you in a while." He smiles happily, but it doesn't reach his eyes. He could be a good guy, but something about him just doesn't sit right with me. Plus, even if he were the greatest guy in the world, it wouldn't matter because he is not my Liam.

"I've been okay, been pretty busy," I tell him. I rub Liam's chest, hoping he will get the hint.

His eyes go to my hand resting on Liam's chest, but he doesn't look at Liam. He just looks at me. This guy either has the biggest pair in the world or plain dumb. I am going with the latter.

"Have you changed your mind about going out?" he asks with a hopeful smile on his face.

Liam laughs loudly, and the guy finally looks at him. His face turns pale, and I look at Liam and see exactly what I expected. He is pissed. It's honestly a huge slap in the face for a guy to approach me in front of my man; it's disrespectful.

He steps back, his hands up. "I didn't know."

"Run," Liam growls.

He turns around and flat-out sprints across the parking lot. Liam laughs loudly and I laugh right along with him.

"The guy was so fucking enraptured with you, he didn't see me until the end." Liam chuckles under his breath, helping me climb into the truck.

He will get over it. "He knows I am taken now." I wink and put on my seatbelt.

Liam wraps his hand around the back of my neck. "That's fucking right, you're mine and will only ever be mine." He kisses me and I twist his shirt in my hands, pulling him closer.

A fingertip touches my inner thigh, and I suck on his lip. My body tenses, waiting for what he is going to do,

His finger stops an inch from my pussy, and I am throbbing with need at this point. "When we get home." He growls, kissing me one last time, and slams the door shut.

I lean against the headrest, looking at the ceiling. If I already want him this badly, just imagine what it is going to be like once we have sex. I kind of hope that is soon. On one hand, it may be too soon but, on the other hand, I have known him since I was sixteen years old and I have wanted him all these years.

I want him and I know he wants me. There is no doubt in my mind that we will be together forever. Some things in life are just meant to be.

He climbs into the truck, the vehicle roaring to life. A shit ton of motorcycles pulls up in the parking lot. The Grim Sinners MC. I see Lane, Wilder, Derek, and a bunch of others running toward the grocery store.

"What the heck is going on?" I ask Liam. He turns the truck off and takes out his phone. My guess is that he's calling Lane.

He is on the phone for a minute or so. "One of the original members got jumped in the grocery store by one of the cartel members."

"Is he okay?"

"Yeah, he is fine—just a few bruises. The original beat his ass." He laughs and starts the truck again. "They don't need my help, and I don't want to expose you to the cartel guys."

He drives out of the parking lot, and I roll down my window and wave to Wilder, who is standing at his bike. I guess the cartel is just hanging around. I don't like them staying silent like they are waiting to attack.

Two places I do feel safe are my house and the club. My house has steel walls that will fall down to cover the house if needed, and you can't get in unless I let you in.

We arrive home a little bit later, after stopping to get some food. As I walk into the house, my phone starts ringing.

"Hello?"

"Hey!" Vanessa whispers into the phone, and I can hear her excitement.

"How was your date?"

Liam strips naked right in front of me, changing into sweats.

Fuck me.

"It's going fabulous, I ran to the bathroom to call you and say thank you. He is hot." She laughs and I hear the water turn on in the background.

"I am so glad you are having a good time!" I tell her. Liam winks at me before walking into the bathroom, his bubble butt out for the world to see.

"I got to go."

"Bye! Have a good time." I hang up the phone and toss it on the counter. Liam walks back into the room, still stark naked.

My eyes immediately go to his dick. He clears his throat and I look up. I blush at the smirk on his face. He walks over, grabs the bottom of my shirt, and pulls it over my head.

I smile at him, laying my hand on his chest. He rests his hand on my jawbone, kissing my forehead. "Liam." I close my eyes, enjoying his presence.

At moments like these, I am taken aback that I have him in my life. Sometimes I just have to take a moment to gather myself.

He kisses my forehead, my cheekbones and, finally, my lips. I shiver and wrap my arms around his shoulders. He grabs my ass and lifts me off the ground, and I wrap my legs around his waist. He bends down with me still in his arms, the bed pressing against my back.

He pulls back and unbuttons my pants, pulling them down my legs right along with my panties. He looks down at me, and I shiver at the heated look on his face. Dear god, this man may kill me. He lifts me off the bed and lays me on his chest. "Ride my face."

Wait, what?

"Liam…" I start to argue, but he smirks, lifts me once more, and settles me over his face. I throw my head back at the amazing feeling, and I grip the headboard. Fingers are buried into my ass cheeks, and he pushes my hips with the movement of his tongue.

My legs are shaking by his head. I am ready to go off at any second. He sits up with me in his arms. I grab the back of his head, and my legs tighten over his shoulders.

His head shakes and I fall over the edge, and I shake so hard I lose my hold on him and start to fall back. I am laid back gently on the bed, and he runs his hands down my body. I want to hold him. I reach up and pull him down so I am cuddling with him.

When do I want to have sex? I feel like it's time because, although I don't want to admit it out loud yet, I do love him. Liam has been my heart for many years. Our finally being together is full proof that I love him, and I love him more each day. There isn't a doubt in my mind.

At the moment he is staring down at my face, running his fingers through my hair so tenderly that there is not a doubt in my mind he loves me too.

"I want you," I whisper and I stiffen, awaiting his answer. Why did I just blurt it out like that? His hand stops in my hair and he stares down at me, his eyes searching my face, and it's my guess is that he is wondering if I am serious.

"Baby, are you sure?" His hand drops from my hair to my face, his thumb stroking my cheekbone.

I twine our fingers together and kiss the back of his hand. "I want you, Liam. It's time."

He smiles beautifully and kisses me deeply, full of passion. He drags his hand down my body and between my legs, his thumb pressed into my clit. I am extra sensitive since my orgasm, and I moan and dig my nails into his back. He kisses me with everything in him. It's like he is trying to pour everything he is feeling into it. He brings me to the brink once again, but he stops when I am about to come. My breathing is ragged and my body stiffens. He brings me to the top of the bed, my head resting on my pillow. He settles between my legs, and I let out a deep breath, feeling nervous because this is a huge deal. It's a bigger deal because it's with him.

"Love, are you sure?" he asks me once more.

I nod my head immediately. "I am sure. I want you, my Liam."

He smiles and presses his forehead against mine, his elbows braced on either side of my head.

I know this is also a big deal for Liam—this is his first time too. We met when he was seventeen and I was sixteen, and we made a commitment to each other. We have only wanted each other, and we've never dated or thought about anyone else.

This is a special moment that will be with us forever.

I run my hands down his back. "You okay with this too, Liam?"

He grins and kisses me. "Baby, I was ready years ago."

I laugh loudly and he lowers his head. I feel his dick at my entrance. I am on birth control and have been since I was thirteen and my periods was unbearable.

Liam isn't a small guy. "Relax, Baby." He rubs my hips, and I lie back into the pillow and relax my body. He slowly starts pressing into me, staring at my face the whole time, and I wince at the feeling of being stretched.

His hand leaves my hips and goes to my clit, his thumb pressing down and circling. I tilt my hips, and he presses into it a little more and sinks in even more. He stops and looks at me and I nod, so he presses forward until I've taken him all the way up to the hilt.

Fuck me. I hide my face in the pillow. I am sure it's not painful for a lot of girls but, mind you, Liam is not a small guy—and when I say he is not small, I mean he is a good eight inches or more and thick.

"Fuck, Paisley, it's killing me that you're hurting," he says harshly and I hear a sound. I look up to see that he has punched the headboard, leaving a dent.

I look at him, his eyes lock on mine, and his face twists in pure horror at the sight of my tears. "Fuck, Baby, I am so sorry." He wipes my tears. He leans forward, his elbows on either side of my face, and kisses my cheek.

"I am okay, Liam, you're not a small guy." I smack his hip and he laughs.

"Now is not the fucking time to inflate my ego."

I laugh harder, he tilts his hips, and I am surprised at how good it feels. "I am good to go."

He moves his hips again, and I lock my legs around them.

He stares down at me, his eyes never leaving mine. I place my hand on his cheek, and he grabs my hand and kisses it.

Who couldn't love him? He is the sweetest guy.

He grinds himself against my clit. I gasp and he moves faster, his hips tilting to hit a spot inside me that has me clenching down on him. I throw my head back, and his finger is back on my clit once again. I clench even tighter, my toes curled. My legs are weak, and I let them fall on the bed.

"Oh my god, Liam," I moan.

He bites my neck, his finger and thumb pinching my clit. I come hard, and he comes hard right along with me.

Our bodies are shaking, and I just hold onto him for dear life. He kisses my neck and strokes my side. I love that he doesn't shy away from showing affection. On the outside you see this huge, badass alpha, but I get this side of him. Only me.

"That was perfect." I hug him.

"You're perfect." He leans up and kisses me.

Yeah, I love him.

six

Paisley

We arrive outside Liam's sister's house. Braelyn adopted him when he moved in with her at seventeen. Liam had a really hard life before he came to live with her.

I hope that I never meet his dad because I would probably beat him badly. In my mind, I just picture a small Liam and his dad beating him.

Pisses me right off.

Liam and I walk hand-in-hand to the front door, which opens, and two little kids run out, Xavier and Samantha, Liam's niece and nephew. Liam lets go of my hand and scoops them both up. He hugs them tightly and Braelyn runs out next, tackling Liam in a hug, and he laughs, picking her up off the ground. Braelyn is just as beautiful as when I met her ten years ago.

He sets her down and she goes straight to me. I hug her back and she smiles at both of us. Liam takes my hand again and her eyes widen, staring at our joined hands.

"About time!" she says loudly and hugs us again, this time with us together. I look at the front door and see Ethan walk out, looking just as beautiful as ever. His hair is graying at the temples, and that makes him ten times hotter, in my opinion.

Ethan has got to be one of the best guys I have ever met, but he is also straight alpha and a police officer. Braelyn came from a shitty background and was homeless for a long time until Ethan took her in.

"Good to see you, Liam, glad you're home." Ethan walks over to Liam and they do the man hug thing.

Braelyn grabs my hand and tugs me into the house, tearing me away from Liam. I look back at him, and he is smirking at me.

Little fucker.

Last night, in a sense, changed everything. We have a deeper connection that I cannot explain and I love it. I love him.

I just want to be around him twenty-four and seven.

Liam

She walks up the stairs to the house with my sister. I stare at her back and it hits me all over again that she is mine.

Last night was the best night of my life. It sealed the fucking deal, and I have wanted her for so long. The wait was worth it ten times over.

"Finally got the girl." Ethan is grinning, his arms across his chest.

"About fucking time," I confess and he laughs, smacking my shoulder. We follow the girls. Xavier and Samantha are already in the house.

Paisley smiles at me when I walk into the kitchen, and it hits me right in the fucking heart because I love this fucking woman and I have for a long-ass time. Sometimes it just hits me how much. Another woman hasn't even crossed my mind. I don't see anyone but her. Everything is blurred but her.

She is my life, my world. My everything.

I am going to marry her ass, have babies, and have a family. I am going to be the dad that I never had. I want it all.

I walk over to her, lift her out of her seat, and kiss her. I kiss her with every fucking thing I have in me. Her hands are twisted into my shirt, giving me back everything I am giving her. I pull back, placing my forehead against her, and look deeply into her eyes, my hand cupping her jaw.

"I fucking love you, Paisley."

Tears fill her eyes immediately. "I love you too, Liam, so much." She kisses me again, her tears falling down her face. I lift her up and place her ass on the counter, my hand buried in her hair, controlling the kiss.

She pulls back and stares at her hand, which is placed over my heart. "I can't believe this all belongs to me," she whispers and falls into my chest. I wrap my arms around her tightly and kiss the top of her head.

"Hey Liam, I think I have something here you might want." I look up to see Ethan holding the vest I made for Paisley years ago.

I take the vest, and she gasps and covers her mouth.

"Be my ole lady?" I wink and she puts on the vest; it fits her perfectly.

"You know it, old man." She winks back and hugs me once again. I look over my shoulder and see that Braelyn is sobbing into Ethan's chest. "That was so beautiful."

"Wait until Torch sees the vest," Ethan says and Paisley freezes, her eyes wide with panic.

"Baby, I don't give a fuck what your dad thinks," I tell her and I don't. Her dad might intimidate a lot of people, but I'm sure as hell not scared of him. "Tonight there is a party at the clubhouse, and you're wearing your vest."

She whispers, "Oh boy."

Paisley

Oh boy is correct. The moment we walked through the front door, everyone turned to stare, and I mean everyone. Hell, I think the music was turned off and everything.

The Grim Sinners MC is here also; we have a full house tonight. My father turns around and his eyes go straight to my vest and Liam's hand, resting on my side. Dad slams down his beer and charges over here, and Liam steps in front of me, ready to take on my father.

Dad stops right in front of Liam, nose to nose. Oh my god, what is going to happen? "What the fuck do you think you're doing?" Dad asks Liam.

I stand beside Liam.

"She is mine, Torch. Don't fucking try to stop this, it won't work."

Dad glares at him. If looks could kill he would be dead ten times over. I walk over and grab Dad's hand. He looks at me, and I can tell that he is sad.

"I will always be your baby, Daddy. I love him," I whisper and Dad closes his eyes, his whole body sinking with defeat.

He pulls me into a hug and the music turns back on. "I love you, baby girl," he says and I hug him tighter.

"I love you, Dad."

Liam pulls me away and holds me against his side. He offers Dad his hand, and Dad stares at it for a few beats before he puts his hand in Liam's. I grin happily and Dad's face softens at my smile.

Dad backs away and Kayla is waiting for him across the room. She hugs him and winks at me over her shoulder. I wave at her; then we are swarmed by everyone in the room. The ole ladies are around me, and the guys are with Liam.

I love this. I love that I am a part of the sisterhood; it's different than just being a princess in the club. This is different. I am a part of the club in a different way. I have a patch.

I look at my family and friends surrounding me, congratulating me. It's hard to believe that, after all of these years, this finally happened.

Liam grabs my hand and I smile and press my head against his shoulder. I love him, and I love my family.

Everything is just perfect and the way it's meant to be.

Until it isn't.

Shit hits the fan.

seven

Paisley

I am exhausted, today has been hell. One after another, things have happened, I was punched in the face by someone who had lost their mind. I have a black eye, and Liam is going to lose his shit.

I walk out of the emergency room, and Liam is waiting for me in the parking lot. I keep my face down, hoping he doesn't see. I know he won't be angry at me or anything like that, but I don't want him upset.

He is a little protective.

"What the fuck happened to your face?" he roars. His hands tilt my face upward, and his face is full of rage.

I grip his forearm. "It was an accident."

He tilts my head to the side, getting a better view of the bruise. "Does it hurt, my love?" He touches the bruises softly.

I smile at how cute he is being. "I am perfectly fine, it was an accident."

His eyes search my face, and I can tell he is trying to make sure that I am telling the truth. He nods, his hand settling on my back.

I hear four car doors slam right behind us, and I turn around and see five men walking toward us. Some of them have weapons, including a baseball bat and steel knuckles.

Oh my god. The cartel.

I look at Liam, full of fear. What will they do? Maybe we can get away? Liam tightens his grip on me and presses me toward the truck. He sticks his hand into his pocket and hands me the truck keys.

"Get inside, lock the doors, and if something happens to me, drive away."

I shake my head. I will not leave him and let these guys hurt him.

"Baby, please, I can't worry about you."

I blink back tears and get into the truck, locking the door. I roll down my window halfway. I open the middle compartment and take out the handgun. I am not fucking leaving.

Liam looks back at me, smiling.

The five guys are standing directly in front of him. I take out my phone and text my dad.

Me: Dad, five cartel members have cornered Liam in the parking lot at the hospital.

I then open the app that was made for the women of the club. I press down the code red button, letting everyone know I need help ASAP.

"Let me have the girl," one of the cartel guys says, and my whole body stiffens with fear. They want me? Why do they want me?

Liam throws his head back laughing, and the five guys look at each other in confusion. Liam looks at all of them. "You came for her?"

"Yes, we did." He steps forward, swinging his bat.

"Big fucking mistake," Liam says, his voice deep with anger.

In the blink of an eye, Liam has the guy's bat out of his hands and is swinging it right at the fucker's head. The guy hits the ground like a ton of bricks. I gape at the sight of him lying there, out cold, with the other guys staring at him.

I would not be surprised if the guy's skull is broken.

Fear is all I feel right now. I fear for Liam, and I fear what could have happened if I had been taken. I don't want to know what they have planned for me.

Two guys attack at once. They look the same, with black T-shirts, jeans, gelled-back hair, and a predatory look.

Liam smashes the butt of the bat into one guy's face. He kicks the other in the stomach, and he hits the ground. Liam swings the bat and hits the one who was trying to sneak out. He hits the ground like the others.

The first two climb back to their feet and the third guy, who is uninjured, comes up behind Liam, trying to grab him from behind. Liam throws out his elbow and hits him.

The other two guys grab Liam at once, one in front of him and one from behind. Liam throws his head back, butting him right in the nose. The guy lets go of Liam and grips his nose, blood pouring out between his fingertips.

Liam grabs the one in front of him, gripping his face between his hands. He pulls his face down as he brings up a knee. I can hear a bone cracking.

Liam picks up his baseball bat, which, somehow, has fallen to the ground, and faces the guy he just kneed in the face. Liam swings the bat, hitting him in the knee. He hits the ground, screaming, and Liam punches him hard in the mouth, shutting him up.

The final guy approaches, and Liam punches him in the jaw. His face twists to the side, and he falls. All of them are on the ground.

My window breaks, a hand reaches in, and I hear the door unlocking. Fear settles in my stomach. The door is swung open, and another one of the cartel members reaches inside.

Liam's face comes into view, tearing the guy away. Liam clutches his hair and smashes his face into the car window right by his truck. Glass breaks around his face, and the guy's body slumps inside the car.

I hear the roar of a shit ton of motorcycles. Then we are surrounded by bikes. My dad is the first one off his bike, and he runs over. Liam reaches inside the truck and scoops me out. I wrap myself around him. Dad stands right beside us and looks at my black eye.

"This was from an accident at work," I reassure him. I look away and tuck my face into the side of Liam's neck.

"Fuck, Liam, did you take all six out yourself?" Techy asks, and I lift my head and look down at the guys on the ground.

"They barely even touched him," I point out. The MC members look at the guys lying on the ground, knocked out, and the one hanging out of a car window.

I close my eyes and bask in the feel of Liam: the warmth, the protection, all that is Liam. I could have lost him today, and that thought is unbearable.

I slowly let myself slide down Liam's body, but he doesn't let me go—he clutches me to his side. His whole body is ready, ready for anything.

"They came for her."

Everyone looks at me, and I can see their angry expressions. Dad grabs the side of his face. "Fuck!" he roars and looks at me, filled with rage and absolute horror.

"Retaliation," Kyle says.

"Fuck yeah," Liam agrees.

A huge black van pulls up beside us, and Tyler, Brett, and Shane climb out of the van. They immediately start loading up the guys.

Tyler looks at me. "You okay, Paisley?"

I nod before answering. "They never touched me, I am fine." Liam kisses the side of my head. I close my eyes, laying my head on his chest.

Dad is standing beside me, and I can tell that he is dying to snatch me away from Liam. I mouth to him, "I am fine, Daddy."

He nods and looks at the ground, his hands clenched into fists. "Go home, Liam, if we need you we will call."

Liam nods and we walk to his truck; he helps me into the truck and climbs in the driver's side. I lift the middle console and sit in the middle, and I buckle up.

"Baby, you okay?" His hand rests on the side of my face that is not lying on his shoulder.

"I am fine, I just want to be close to you right now, Baby," I confess and he strokes the side of my face.

I watch the traffic all around us. Liam's body is still tight, ready for anything. I just want to be home; I want to be held and in my bed, where I feel safe.

You would think that, as an MC kid, I would be used to this kind of thing, but I am not. I have seen some shit, but I'm not used to being directly affected by the MC's battles. I was protected from all this. But today, they gunned for me.

They were planning on kidnapping me and doing god knows what. Liam took on six men and didn't have a scratch on him. I never realized how much of a badass and a dangerous person he is until this very moment. Liam was always badass, but I was up close and personal to see how truly dangerous he is.

He is a beast.

Liam

They came for her. They sent six fucking men to take her from me, and these guys are suffering the consequences.

It would take a hell of a lot to take her away from me. I would fight, kill, and do whatever it takes to keep her with me.

She is mine, she is my woman and my life. My life is not being taken from me.

I grip the steering wheel hard, the leather creaking under my grip. I will kill every single one of these motherfuckers and make them pay for what they have done.

This shit will end, and fucking soon—there is no doubt about that.

Paisley

An Hour Later

Liam and I are both showered, in bed, and watching TV. I don't think either of us is really watching though. Our minds are going a million miles an hour.

"Paisley, I hate that someone was coming for you." His hand stops on the middle of my back, and I look at him.

"I am fine, Liam. You protected me."

He sure did protect me—he protected me in a fierce way that I have never seen before. I have never seen him so angry; he was vicious. They never even hit him, it was wild.

"I wish those fuckers were dead," he says through clenched teeth.

I snuggle against him, my fingers digging into his chest. He hugs me tighter. I honestly don't know what to say to him. I wish these people were out of my life, out of my family's life.

This town is our safe haven; I grew up here and have always felt safe because the MC keeps out these kinds of people. We do what we have to do, just like the Grim Sinners MC. The cartel is trying to take out the small coastal towns, and we can't allow that to happen. I don't want this town to be swallowed up by drugs.

Liam's phone rings and he picks it up. I hear someone talking but I can't hear what they are saying.

He hangs up the phone, stares at the ceiling for a few minutes, and looks at me. "I have to go to the club."

I know exactly what he has to do. I nod and climb out of bed, and I slip on my clothes. Liam does the same, putting his gun on his hip.

He grabs my hand and we go out to his truck, which has been reinforced, like my car, with bulletproof windows and other safety features. The Grim Sinners and Devil Souls MCs don't like to take any chances, and their tech guys often team up on developing safety features.

We sit in silence on the way to the club. I stare at Liam. I can tell he is still pissed, mainly because he is about to tear the steering wheel off; the leather is cracking.

The gate opens when we reach the club and, the moment we are inside, the door slams shut immediately, not leaving a second for someone to slip through.

We walk inside the club, and Shaylin is sitting on the couch with her daughter. Liam kisses the side of my head and walks back to the interrogation room.

Shaylin looks at me. "You okay, honey?" She lifts Tiana, cuddling her against her chest. The little girl's eyes are sleepy.

"I am fine." I smile and touch Tiana's cheek. She is one of the most beautiful toddlers I have ever seen. I was there the moment she became a part of Shaylin and Butcher's life. She had been left in a car where her mother had overdosed. The mother hated Shaylin, but Shaylin took in the little girl.

She had it rough until Shaylin and Butcher came into her life; now she has Butcher wrapped around her little finger. Butcher is this huge beast of a dude who is meaner than fuck, except when it comes to Shaylin and Tiana.

An hour passes. Tiana is asleep, lying on the couch beside Shaylin and me. The men are still in the back room.

My phone buzzes in my pocket, and I take it out and see a text from Vanessa. "I am outside the gate, can you let me in?"

What the hell? What is she doing here? She has never been here. *Oh my goodness, do you think the cartel is after her?* "My friend is outside the gates, I am going to see what's wrong."

Shaylin nods and smooths Tiana's hair out of her face.

I open the door and look out into the lot but, at first glance, I don't see Vanessa. Weird, where is her car? I walk closer to the gate and look through the bulletproof glass.

I don't see her anywhere. This is really unusual for her. "Vanessa?" I call out to her but all I get is silence.

Something is seriously wrong.

I turn around. I need to tell Liam what is happening. What if she is lying out there or the cartel has her?

Something wet hits the top of my shoulder and falls down my back.

Pain, intense pain.

I scream and touch my back, and my hand immediately starts burning. I scream louder as the pain gets worse and worse.

What is happening? My legs give out and I hit the ground hard. I smell something god awful.

I look at the door to the clubhouse; Shaylin is standing there looking at me in horror. I scream again, the pain sinking in and becoming worse.

It's like my whole back is on fire, it hurts so bad.

I am dying, the world is getting darker around the edges. Shaylin runs to me and hits the ground, and she touches my face. Her mouth is moving, but I don't hear a sound.

I close my eyes.

Darkness.

eight

Liam

I finish pulling out the final fingernail on the last guy, making sure I get all of the information I need. About an hour has passed. I have gone through four of them, and all of them have spilled their guts.

The stupid fuckers tried to keep all of this shit hidden, but they hadn't faced me. I was trained for this, and there is nothing I can't get out of somebody. I can keep someone alive for days, weeks, and even months.

They all crack.

The door is thrown open, and one of the old ladies looks at us in pure terror. Then I hear it.

A scream, a scream that I will never get out of my head. A scream that I know.

Paisley.

I run out of the room with Torch at my back. I look around the main room, knowing she is outside. I throw open the door and see Shaylin on her knees by Paisley.

My Paisley.   The lower part of her back is burned. Liquid is on the ground behind her, and I fucking know it's acid.

Pain, that's the only way I can explain how I feel. It's like my heart is being ripped out of my chest. "Call 911!" I yell at the top of my lungs, my heart ripping in fucking two.

"Paisley," I choke out. My heart hurts so fucking bad. She doesn't wake up. Torch falls next to me. "Baby, please." My head falls, and my hand is shaking so fucking bad. I push her hair out of her face. "What the fuck happened!" I roar.

Shaylin looks at me, tears rolling down her face. "She got a text from her friend, she said she was outside the gate," she whispers.

The fucking cartel.

I don't know what to do. I am helpless. I lie down on the ground beside her, and I kiss her cheek and pray. *Please don't take her away, she is my life.* Torch is holding her hand.

A few achingly slow minutes tick by before the ambulance shows up and the gate opens, allowing them inside. The paramedics run over, horror all over their fucking faces at the sight of her.

We slowly move her onto the gurney. Maybe it's a fucking blessing she's out cold. Her back is burned, bad. Really fucking bad.

I get onto the ambulance with her, and Torch gets in beside me. My eyes never leave her face. She is still out.

"They are dead," Torch says.

"You are damn fucking right."

I am going to track them down, one by one, and destroy them.

Paisley

When I open my eyes, the first thing I see is Liam, and the next thing I notice is my back is really fucked up; the pain is bad. Liam scoots forward and touches my cheek. "Baby." He lowers his head, his breathing harsh.

I try to scoot closer, and I cry out in pain. His head shoots up, and he stops me from moving. "Stop, Baby, your back."

I stop, remembering everything that happened. Someone threw something over the gate and it hit my back. "How bad is it, Liam?"

He lets out a deep breath. "It's not seriously bad, but it's on the top of your hips and the small of your back. It's severe third-degree burns."

I close my eyes. The feeling of it hitting my back is something I will never forget. "Vanessa?" I ask, almost afraid to know what happened.

"Someone stole her phone from work."

I cover my face, crying into my hands, because I can't believe this happened. I want to be strong for Liam, but I don't want to be strong right now.

I was burned. Someone threw acid on me. They didn't intend to kill me, but they hurt me in a way that will affect me forever.

"Paisley." Liam kisses my cheek and puts his hand on the top of my shoulder. "I am so fucking sorry, Baby, I wish I could take it from you."

"It's not your fault, Liam, I am just emotional right now."

He kisses my temple once more, his hand drifting through my hair.

"Sleep, my love, I will be right here." His fingers stroke my hair and the top of my back, soothing me. My body is shaking; I guess it's from the pain and shock.

Liam

Her hand is on my forearm, and I stare down into her sleeping face; it's so peaceful. I look down at her back, seeing the raw, burned skin. She is going to be scarred and, honestly, I feel like it's my fault.

I wasn't there to protect her, and that shit is eating away at my fucking core. It's my job to make sure she is safe.

Her body is still shaking, even in sleep, and she is running a slight fever. I grab a blanket and cover her legs.

The door opens, and Torch walks in with Kayla, returning from the cafeteria. His eyes are only on his daughter.

"She woke up for a few minutes."

Torch closes his eyes, relieved. Kayla's face is red with tears. She rubs her eyes and sits down beside me.

Everyone is affected by this shit; she is a huge part of everyone's lives. Paisley brings happiness to everyone around her, and she is so fucking strong. Even when she is hurt she worries about me.

She is fucking beautiful, inside and out.

"Maybe she should move in with us for a while, so we can take care of her," Kayla suggests, pissing me the fuck off.

I look at her. "I will take care of her."

She looks at me, her face sad. "She is going to need a lot of help, for a while, doing everything."

I look away because this shit is just words; nobody is taking care of her but me. I know what it will take, and I will do it all. She is mine. I will always take care of her, no matter what. "I will take care of her, she is my woman."

She doesn't say anything. It wouldn't do her any fucking good because this shit is final.

Paisley

A Few Days Later

"Fuck." I sit up in bed. I bite the back of my hand trying not to cry out; this is painful. It's on the sides of my hips and lower back. When I move, my back moves—making my burns hurt.

I need to use the bathroom, badly.

Liam wakes up. "Baby, why didn't you wake me?" He gets out of the chair he was asleep in. He has not left me; he has been by my side the whole time I've been at the hospital. I look down at the floor. I hate that he has to help me do everything.

"Paisley, what's wrong, Baby?" He's on his knees in front of me, cupping my face.

"I hate that you have to help me," I whisper to him.

His face softens. "Baby, never feel like that. I want nothing more than to take care of you." He looks me right in my eye. "I love you, so much. I want to take care of you, you're my woman."

I smile and kiss him, and he kisses me back. I lift my arms slowly and put them around his shoulders, and he grabs the bottom of my ass, lifting me from the bed slowly. My legs are on either side of his hips.

He carries me to the bathroom; then he gently sets me on my feet and slides down my pants along with my underwear. I hide my face, embarrassed.

"Don't do that shit, Paisley." He slowly helps me down onto the toilet and leaves, giving me privacy.

I can't help but feel that way. I'm so used to taking care of myself, and now I can't. That shit is tough to deal with.

I finish and wash my hands in the sink by the toilet. It's a slow, painful process, because I have to bend my back. Liam comes back into the bathroom once the water is shut off. He puts his hands under my armpits, lifting me off the toilet so I don't strain myself, trying to cause the least amount of pain possible.

A chemical burn is the worst kind of pain. The acid burned layers of skin, and the burn is in a bad place because my skin twists and bends in that area.

We slowly make our way back to the bed, and I lie on my stomach. Liam made the hospital bring in another bed, and he lies beside me.

He turns off the light; it's nighttime now. He fell asleep in the chair right before I decided to go to bed for the night. He gets on the other bed, which is pressed up against mine. He covers most of my body with the blanket I made Dad bring from home, careful not to lay it on my burned skin. Then he lays another over the top of my back and arms.

"I love you too, Liam, so much. Thank you for doing this," I whisper, and I grab his hand and kiss the back of it.

"I love you too, my love."

My stomach flips when the butterflies hit me. I love him so much, and that is the truth. My every thought is about him.

He puts his hand on the back of my neck, his fingers on my pulse. He has been doing this since the accident. I asked him why, and he said it assures him I am here and okay.

"Goodnight," I whisper and drift off to sleep.

nine

Three Months Later

Liam

I kick in the door, and the cartel members spring off the couch in shock. I smile, seeing the pure fear all over their fucking faces.

For the past couple of weeks, I have hunted and hunted, taking down every single member I can find.

I shut the door behind me. They stare at me for a few beats; then they bolt. I laugh at the sight of their pure terror. I love that shit, I want to bathe in that. They fucked with Paisley, and I will take out every fucker I possibly can.

I raise my gun, aiming at the back of the closest cartel member. I pull the trigger, and he hits the ground with a thump. Pure happiness is what I fucking feel. The fewer of them walking this earth the better. Paisley went through hell getting over her burns.

They will pay and they are paying.

I hear the back door open, and I grin because they are going to get a surprise. I follow them to the door.

Tyler, Shane, and Brett are waiting for them, guns aimed at their heads. One of the members steps back and bumps into my chest. He slowly turns around, his eyes wide with fear, and I grin. I slam my fist onto his mouth, and he hits the ground.

The other two guys spin around, and I shoot the one on the left. I grab the other by the back of the neck, slamming his face into the wall. The wall breaks, and his head is inside it. I let him go and leave him just hanging there. Tyler looks at the sky, pretending to be bored. "I didn't get to do anything."

I roll my eyes. "These fuckers are mine to kill." I laugh at his pissed-off look.

It killed me to see her hurt, and there was nothing I could do to stop the pain.

I took care of her and wiped away her tears, and these fuckers will pay for every tear she shed. They attacked the club where it hurt, and Torch has been a fucking mess—he has been at Paisley's house every day.

My phone rings in my pocket. I take it out and see it's Paisley. "Hello."

"What do you want for dinner?" she asks me. I can hear her moving around in the background.

"Doesn't matter, Baby, whatever you want."

She sighs into the phone. "Well, I hope you're having a good day with the boys."

I look at the guys on the floor; some of them are passed out and others are dead. I smile before answering her. "I am having a blast."

Tyler laughs and begins dragging the bodies out of the house. The ones that are alive will get a special visit from me, and I will get info on other cartel members. I will be picking these fuckers off until there are none left.

Torch walks into the hallway where I am standing, and he has one of the cartel guys over his shoulder. He bends down and the guy hits the ground, a bullet planted between his eyes. He smiles at me. "Missed one."

In the past few months we have come to an understanding that Paisley is the most important thing in our lives. He tolerates me, and I still don't give a fuck what he thinks.

"I need to get this shit cleaned up, I got to see my woman." I look at Torch pointedly. He glares at me and points his gun at me, and I grin.

I take out my gun and point it right the fuck back. He grunts and walks away.

That's fucking right.

Paisley

If it's possible, I fell more in love with Liam every single day while I was recuperating. My getting hurt has brought us closer together.

He took care of me. I felt like a burden at first, but he shut me up really quick when I started to feel bad.

He did everything he could possibly have done for me. I'd never felt more loved or taken care of. What happened to me affected me emotionally. I used to be independent, and I had to have help with everything.

Bending down was the worst. It pulled at my burns, and that was painful—beyond painful, actually.

I also find it hilarious that my father and Liam have fought over me through the whole healing process, and they are still doing it, even now that I am better. Liam just smiles at Dad like he is the most hilarious person in the world, and that bugs my dad more than anything.

We are having dinner at his house tomorrow night, and that is going to be an entertaining night. That might be an understatement.

Tyler and Vanessa are now a full-blown couple, and they have to be the most gorgeous couple I have ever seen. I have never seen her happier than she has been with him. He has brought out the best in her.

Next week there will be a party, but it's more than that. It's usually a two-year process for prospects to get into the club, but Tyler, Shane, and Brett have proven themselves, over and over, to be reliable members.

They are getting patched in, and it's a total surprise; I can't wait to see their faces. But it's also Liam's surprise birthday party. He thinks it's just a surprise patch-in.

Boy, is he clueless. I have been planning this, and I have bought him the one thing he has wanted for years.

He has been searching for this bike for years, and there were not any for sale until I got Techy on the job. He found someone who was selling one in the next state. They are bringing it, and Kyle is keeping it at his house until the day of the party. He is going to bring it over and hide it until it's time to give it to Liam.

The front door opens and Liam comes into the living room and takes off his shoes. Biting my lip, I slip off all of my clothes. I cover my mouth to stop my giggle and walk straight to our bedroom. I can hear him chasing me, and laughter is bubbling up in my stomach, which is filled with excitement.

An arm bands around my waist, and I am lifted off the ground and thrown onto the bed. Liam is stripping off his clothes.

I look up and down his beautiful body. It should be a crime for someone to look like this. He is just perfect, and he is perfect on the inside too. He has the best heart; well, maybe only when it comes to me.

He has a slight temper.

"Hey, Baby," I say. I lean up and push my hair out from under my back. His eyes lock onto my naked body. "How was your day?"

"Way fucking better now," he growls, falling to his knees. His hands wrap around my calves, pulling me down the bed. I throw my legs over his shoulders, and his head is between my legs.

"Goodness!" I hiss, my hands twisting in his hair. He growls, his hands tightening and pulling me harder against his mouth. His mouth is licking, sucking, and nipping in all of the right places, places that drive me wild.

"Fuck me, Liam," I beg.

I've been wanting him like crazy all day long. I crave him like he is my next breath. His hands go to my hips, and he turns me so my back is facing him. He lifts my hips and I lean on my elbows.

Lips press against my burn scars. I grit my teeth, my eyes clenched closed, trying not to cry even though he has done this many times. The first time he saw my scars, I was self-conscious. He made it his mission to ensure that I wasn't self-conscious and that I knew he loved all of me, scars and all.

One thing I will never doubt is his love for me. I don't know what I ever did to deserve someone like him, but I thank God every single day that I have him.

I feel him at my entrance, and I push back as he pushes in all the way to the hilt. I groan and push back harder, circling my hips. His fingers are tight around my hips, controlling our movements.

He slides out and back in, slowly. My whole body shivers at the pure pleasure. "Feel good, Baby?" he asks, his hand rubbing my ass cheek, down to my clit, which he pinches.

My whole body jolts. I clench around him, and that is when he lets loose, giving me all he has, pounding into me hard. His hips slam against me with every thrust.

I clutch the sheet, biting it as I try not to scream. His hand slides up my back, then into my hair. I look back and he grabs my hair, turning my head so I'm looking at him.

His eyes bore into mine, and he slams home, our hips twisting, and his free hand rolls my clit. My eyes roll back into my head, and I come hard around his dick, my whole body shaking with the aftershocks.

He comes right along with me, and I fall face first onto the bed, breathing hard. Liam pushes my hair out of my face, and he slowly pulls out of me and settles down beside me, pulling me onto his chest.

"Love you, Liam."

He smiles, kissing my cheek. "I love you too, my love."

ten

"Get your hands off of her, Liam, before I shoot your ass," Dad says for the tenth time since we have walked into the house.

"Dad, he is just touching my shoulder."

His eyes widen like I am the crazy one. "So what, he is touching you." His fists are clenched on top of the table.

Liam's hand drifts from my shoulder and down my arm, and he smiles at my father. He is doing it on purpose, that little fucker. My father's face reddens. Liam isn't making it better, that's for sure. I hear Kayla laughing from the kitchen, and I know that she is eavesdropping.

We have finished eating, but Liam is eating his third helping of dessert. I pick up my plate and leave them to their own devices.

Kayla is leaning against the counter, her hand pressed against her mouth, trying to hold in her laughter. She looks at me, tears falling from her eyes. I laugh at her, and she drops her hand and lets her laughter out. "I love every minute of this, your dad always likes to tease me that my boy will have a girlfriend someday."

Kayla has become a mother figure to me. She came into my life when I was nineteen, and we just clicked from the beginning. My father never had a girlfriend until I was out of the house and on my own.

Kayla was blind when I first met her. She had surgery to correct the problem with her eyes, and now she can see.

When was she was blind, she was really independent. She wanted to do everything on her own.

In the end she was the best thing that ever happened to my father. I have never seen him happier.

Kayla smiles at me. "Your father just loves you, and you're his baby girl. He can't help but feel this way."

"I know why he feels this way. He is my daddy, and I love him. I want him to get along with Liam. I want us to be a huge family. Liam is not going anywhere."

"You've been in love with him so long, and he has been in love with you too. You're what everyone strives for— you're what love is."

I smile happily at her kind words, and I walk over and hug her tightly. She gives the kind of hugs that only a mother can give.

"They have been awful quiet, we better check on them," Kayla says and we walk back into the dining room.

Liam

Paisley walks into the kitchen with Kayla, and I look at Torch, who is staring holes through me. He gets up; then I feel the gun pressed to the back of my head. "I should kill you for touching her."

I set the fork down on my plate. "Motherfucker, you have two seconds to get that off the back of my head, before I make you eat it."

Torch doesn't move for a second, and before I can stand up, he takes the gun away. I look at him. "Torch, you can do whatever the fuck you want with me, but she is my woman. I love her, you can't take her away."

Torch stares at me for a few beats. "She is my daughter," he says and falls back into his seat, staring at me.

I push my plate away. "I know she is your daughter. I have to admit that if I had a daughter I would be doing the same thing, if not worse. I love your daughter, man, and I will take care of her. She will always be your daughter, but she is my woman."

Torch stares at me for a few beats and then sinks further into his chair. He is giving in. This shit needed to end. I am tired of the fucker trying to kill me.

He gets the last word in. "Take care of her or you die."

I laugh. I don't blame him one bit because I am sure I would be the same way if I had a daughter. Especially if she looked anything like Paisley. I am not sure I would be as nice as Torch, and the fucker has given me hell. I would probably kill the guy, to be honest.

The girls walk into the room, and they look at me and Torch. I guess they're wondering if they missed anything. Paisley's phone starts ringing and she answers.

"Hey Vanessa!" Her face drops as she talks on the phone. I get out of my chair and walk over to her.

"I am on my way." Paisley hangs up, and I touch her side to get her attention. "Vanessa's dad showed up and beat her up. Tyler is on a rampage."

Fuck.

"Let's go." I take her hand and pull her out of the house while she yells "goodbye" over her shoulder.

We get to Vanessa's and go into her house. I gasp immediately at the sight of her face, my stomach sinking.

It's in bad shape. Her lip is busted and bleeding. Her cheekbone is split, along with her eyebrow, and the rest of her is bruised and covered in blood. Tyler is sitting beside her, holding her, but her face is pointed in my direction. He looks at us, pissed off beyond belief. I don't blame him. My blood is boiling. I take out my phone and call Shaylin because if you're in the mood to beat some ass she is the one to call.

"Hello?"

"Vanessa's dad came to visit her, and he beat her up, want to go beat some ass?" I smile at the sound of her running through the house.

"Fuck yeah, I am getting the girls together. Meet you at the club in an hour." She hangs up. Vanessa is staring at me in utter shock.

I sit down beside her, taking her hand. Her nails are torn from hitting him back. The fucker has always liked to beat up on his kids, and it is time for him to learn his lesson.

I look at Tyler. "You will get your turn once I have my fun. Vanessa needs to go to the hospital. He will be at the club waiting on you."

He smiles. Liam presses his hand on my shoulder, and I look up to see him grinning at me evilly. It's time for some fun. We girls let the men handle a lot of shit, but when it's personal, we band together and give back tenfold.

Vanessa has tears running down her face.

"Why don't you come stay with me and Liam for a while?"

She shakes her head and looks at Tyler.

"She is staying with me from now fucking on." His voice is deep with anger.

Vanessa pushes her hair out of her face, her hands shaking badly. "He wanted money and I didn't have any cash on me," she whispers, looking down at the rug.

Tyler grinds his jaws together, his head turned away from her so she doesn't see. I hate her father. He is a mean fucker who has done nothing but make her life a living hell. "He will never bother you again, we will make sure of it."

She smiles at me weakly. She is the most humble and sweetest person I have ever met. She is the kind of person who would take off her shoes and give them to a homeless person. I have seen it with my own eyes. To see this happen to her is heartbreaking.

I get off the couch, bend down, and hug her gently. "I will get your revenge," I whisper in her ear and she nods, squeezing my hand. Liam intertwines his fingers with mine, and we walk out to the truck and Liam helps me inside. I look through the window of Vanessa's house to see her crying into Tyler's chest. It breaks my heart all over again.

Liam gets in the truck and looks through the window with me. "I don't understand how a man can put his hands on a woman, let alone his own daughter." Liam shakes his head. "Baby, there are some fucked-up people in this world who have no heart."

He starts the truck and leaves for the club.

"I am going to have some fun." I grin into the darkness. I am not the most violent person, but I am very protective of those I care about.

"He will get his, Baby."

Yes, he will.

Paisley

The fucker is in the bar the club owns, drinking and having the best time of his life. The girls and I walk over to him.

The guys did not let us go alone, but they are hanging back. It's a just in case thing, but they won't be needed.

"Hey," I say to Vanessa's dad.

He turns around, and his eyes light up at the sight of me. Vomit crawls up the back of my throat. "Well, aren't you pretty."

I smile at him and slip on my steel knuckles. "Yeah? You think so?"

He licks his lips, nodding.

"Well, I don't think you're pretty, not one bit. Maybe I can help you."

His eyes widen in confusion right before I slam my fist right into his mouth. His head swings back. He holds his mouth, finally noticing the rest of the girls. "Who the fuck are you, all of you?"

"Your worst fucking nightmare. Vanessa is the property of the Devil Souls, and this is your punishment," I inform him as Shaylin brings her bat down on his knee, grinning ear-to-ear. The sound of the bone breaking radiates through the room. She is Smiley's daughter, that is for sure.

Jean laughs and Tases the fucker right between the legs. His face reddens, veins sticking out on the side of his neck, before he hits the floor, screaming.

Jean laughs loudly and high fives all the girls. I join in, still pissed off that this happened to Vanessa. It makes me sick that someone thinks they can put their hands on a woman, let alone their child. I don't understand, I will never understand, why anyone would hurt someone they are supposed to care about. The thought of saying anything mean to Liam breaks my heart.

I stare down at the man who, hours before, beat his daughter badly because she didn't give him money. He is a waste of space.

I hear the guys laughing behind us, watching in pure delight. These are guys you don't want to fuck with. I learned that from an early age. But never once have they raised their voices to me or been mean to me; they are my family. They have protected me and babysat me and my best friends. We had sleepovers. The MC president, Kyle, had tea parties with me. He would kill me if I told anyone that though. I give Kyle a smile, which he returns. He is a mean fucker, that is for sure, but I have seen his soft side. A soft side that many haven't seen. Butcher took me to the park and played Barbies with me. Now all of these men have families of their own, and I know they are the best.

Especially my dad; he is the best dad. I may not have had a mom, but he filled the role as best he could. When I started my period and was scared out of my mind, he bought me what I needed, dried my tears, and babied me.

When I was sick, he slept on the couch with me, holding me all night long just in case I needed him. He taught me how to ride a bike and shoot a gun, and he is my best friend. I hate that he was so torn up because of Liam, but I also know that, deep down, he likes Liam.

"I am sorry!" Vanessa's dad cries out. I tear my gaze from my dad, who is staring right back at me.

I bend down, looking Vanessa's dad right in the face. "Sorry doesn't mean anything, are you sorry we are hurting you or that you hurt your daughter?"

He stares at me, anger replacing his fear, and he sits up quickly and wraps his hand around my throat. His fingers squeeze hard, and I grip his forearm, trying to tear his hand away. Arms band around my waist and Liam is there, punching the guy hard in the face.

Vanessa's father lets go and falls back against the floor. I gasp loudly, trying to catch my breath. Kayla looks at me, her eyes filled with absolute horror, and touches my throat.

"I am okay."

Liam

Rage. Rage hits me hard at the sight of the fucker with his hands wrapped around her throat and the panic and pain on her face.

Torch wraps his arm around her waist, and I punch the fucker hard in the face. He hits the ground hard, hitting his head, and Shaylin puts her foot on his throat, stopping him from getting back up.

Paisley is holding her throat. After Kayla steps back, I put my hands on her face. "Baby, you hurt?"

She shakes her head. "I am okay." She falls forward, her head hitting the middle of my chest. I look over my shoulder at the guys. They pick the guy up off the floor and drag him out of the bar.

"Kick his ass for me." She smiles at me.

"You don't have to fucking ask." I wink and I feel someone staring at me. It is her father, looking fucking torn. I can tell he wants to be the one to comfort her right now.

She follows my gaze and sees her father. I drop my arms and she goes straight to him. She was his life for years and years, until Kayla came into his life, and he's having a hard time letting go.

If I had a daughter, I wouldn't be so fucking nice. My daughter will never have a boyfriend. She will be my baby forever.

Tyler shows up a couple of hours later with Vanessa. He settles her down on the couch, and the ladies start fussing over her immediately. Paisley is looking at her, worried, Vanessa looks like she is still in shock. Tyler walks over to me, his fists clenched at his sides.

"She has a mild concussion—but, besides that, just bruising. She is quiet, man, why the fuck would someone hurt her like that? She is the sweetest person I have ever met." He looks torn into a million fucking pieces.

Tyler is a tough son of a bitch. He has been from the moment I met him all of those years ago. He never had a lot of good in his life until Vanessa gave him a small slice of it.

Then the fucker came along and damaged that.

I understand that, because of Paisley. She is my life, and the thought of someone hurting her kills my fucking soul.

Vanessa's father wrapped his hands around her throat, and I saw the split second of fear on her face. That shit haunts my dreams. My childhood never keeps me up at night, but the sight of her fear, the look on her face when she was burned, and the weeks it took her to get better— that shit killed me. I wanted to take her pain away and make it my own. My woman should never feel pain like that.

She is my Paisley.

Tyler walks back to the interrogation room, where the rest of the guys wait. "The fucker choked Paisley, I need a piece too."

Tyler nods immediately. He will get the kill.

We walk into the room. The guy's arms are above his head, in chains. I have been in this room many times before, and our target is always in the same position.

I was trained in interrogation. I was sent off once I hit eighteen and learned everything I needed to know to get information that could save the club. It is what I did in the SEALs. This is what I fucking do. Today I'm not getting information. I am beating someone's ass.

The guy looks at us. His face is pale and sweat is pouring down his face. This fucker is a piece of shit, the worst kind of man in the entire world, the kind who hurts a woman, even his own fucking kid.

His face goes snow white at the sight of me walking toward him. I take down his right hand. The same hand that choked Paisley. It is grimy, soiled with all kinds of nasty shit that I don't want to think about. He tries to wrench his hand away, but I hold on tight.

"You think you can choke my woman and get away with it?" I ask him.

His whole body is shaking. "I didn't mean to hurt her." His voice is shaking right along with his body.

I smile. "Yeah, well that shit doesn't matter anyway." I grab his fingers and press them back slowly. Farther and farther. His screams pierce the room, and I grin. Then I hear the popping sound of all of his fingers breaking, and his screams grow louder.

I wrap my hands around his wrist and wrench it to the side, breaking it right along with his fingers.

"Watch your shoe, Liam," Kyle says and I look down. Wetness is pooling at his feet. The fucker pissed himself.

I bring up my knee and break his elbow. His face falls forward as he passes out. His whole body is hanging by one hand.

I step back and Tyler brings a bucket of water and splashes it in his face. He wakes up with a start and looks down at his mangled hand.

Tyler steps in front of him, rolling his shoulder. "Vanessa is my woman, you have hurt her for the last fucking time, and don't think I don't know what you did to her when she was little."

Tyler looks behind him. "This shit does not leave this room. I was about to track him down, but the fucker came here and did this shit. The fucker likes to touch little girls, including his own daughter."

This changes the whole fucking game. The whole room changes ten degrees because we are no longer going to just beat this fucker's ass and be done.

No, this fucker is going to be tortured. He is not going to die easy.

Tyler smiles. "Who is ready for some fun?"

An hour has passed, and there is nothing left to do to the fucker but kill him. His arms are broken, there isn't a tooth left in his fucking mouth, and his face resembles ground beef.

He deserved every second of it. I knew Vanessa had a rough go of it, but I had no idea how bad it was. Looking him right in the face makes me sick to my stomach.

Kyle hands Tyler a gun, and Tyler presses the barrel to his head. Vanessa's dad is looking at Tyler, accepting his fate. "Go to hell," he tells Tyler.

Tyler throws his head back, laughing. "Well, I will see you there. The devil has a special fucking place for someone like you."

He pulls the trigger.

Kyle takes the gun and smacks him on the back. "Your woman will breathe easy now knowing he is out of her life."

Tyler nods and lets out a deep breath; then he walks to the bathroom we use for cleaning up. Blood covers his arms and the front of his shirt. "I will call the clean-up crew, let's all go home," Kyle tells everyone and they file out. I walk into the bathroom and find Tyler staring at himself in the mirror.

"It fucking kills me the life she had," Tyler tells me.

"She will have a better one now, man. She won't have that fear wearing on her anymore. All you can fucking do is protect and love them."

He doesn't reply.

I go to another sink and clean up. I don't want Paisley to see all of this shit covering me. She knows what went on in this room, but she doesn't need a firsthand look at all of it.

I want to keep Paisley from all of this. I don't want the darkness to touch her. I just hate that it has touched her at all and that she's had a glimpse of what people are capable of.

I walk back into the main room, which is half a living room. Vanessa's head is on Paisley's lap, and a blanket is covering her.

Tyler scoops Vanessa up out of her lap. "Thank you, Paisley." Tyler carries Vanessa right out of the clubhouse, and Paisley watches them leave.

"Let's go home." She looks at me, taking my hand. She smiles and moves to my side.

Right where she belongs.

eleven

Paisley

Today is the day that Tyler, Shane, and Brett are getting patched, and we are also celebrating Liam's birthday, which is tomorrow. His bike got here yesterday, and Kyle is putting it in one of the rooms at the club. When the time is right, he will bring it out for me. I can't wait to see Liam's face; he has wanted this for years. I had to bribe the guy a lot to get him to sell it, but I got that accomplished.

I am also giving Liam the key to my house. Even though he has been staying with me since he got back, I want him to have that key so it's set in stone.

I walk into the club and Liam goes off to the side with the other guys. I head to the kitchen. I get a text, and I take out my phone.

Shaylin: I am here, open the kitchen door.

I run over to the door that leads to the back of the club. I push it open, and Shaylin walks inside with Liam's huge birthday cake. Chrystal has the refrigerator open, and Shaylin slides the cake inside.

I can't wait to see his face. Braelyn and Ethan will be here later, not that Liam knows that.

Liam has had a few birthday parties since he got to Braelyn's, but nothing big like this because that is not what he wanted. But I don't give a shit what he wants because I am going to give him this.

It kills me on the inside when I think about what kind of childhood he had. It was horrible. I know that he never had enough food to eat, and he had a steady rotation of pimps and drug dealers in his house. He watched his mother get beaten and I don't want to know what else. When he got older, he tried to step between his mother and these guys, but that led to him getting beaten up. That breaks my heart. I picture a small Liam, scared, hiding in a corner, witnessing all of this going down.

He never had that motherly love, and he never had a real father. The father he did have beat him and Braelyn every single day. Braelyn had it rough. I am not sure how she got over what a shitty hand she was dealt, but she is one of the strongest people I have ever met.

Vanessa has been doing a lot better. She knows that her father is dead, and she is okay with it. She told me that she was relieved; she was tired of looking over her shoulder. She can finally be happy and free with Tyler.

I haven't gotten to see many of the new guys getting patched into the club, and it's almost unheard of for three to be patched in at a time. Most prospects don't make it this far.

Kyle walks into the kitchen and waves me over. I follow him into the main room, and we sneak past Liam toward the back of the club. Kyle pushes the door open, and I see the sleek black beast of a bike. I smile and walk closer to it. "He is going to be so surprised!" I tell Kyle.

"Fuck yeah! That's one hell of a bike," Kyle tells me.

He is not wrong. It's the most beautiful bike that I have ever seen. "Thank you for helping me, Kyle."

His face softens. Kyle has been my uncle since I was a little girl. This is the guy who had tea parties with me.

"Anything for you, sweetheart. I am glad to see you're happy, and I don't give a fuck if Liam is a brother or not, if he doesn't make you happy, I will kill him."

I snort before laughing loudly. "Kyle, we both know Liam would never do anything like that, and we both know you're a softy."

He glares at me. "I am fucking not."

I laugh louder. "I remember the tea parties, Kyle."

His face falls, and I laugh louder at the sight of his shocked face. I never brought it up before. It's some kind of code to never bring up anything like that since it would bruise his badass image.

I slip past him and run away, with him on my ass.

"Keep your trap shut, Paisley."

I laugh louder, running into the main room.

Everyone turns to look at me and Kyle. The president who barely speaks, let alone laughs, is running after me, laughing. It's a shocking sight.

Liam steps out from behind the table, and I run over and hide behind him. Kyle stands in front of Liam, laughing.

"What the fuck is going on? Who drugged Kyle?" Techy muses and Kyle's face drops, glaring at Techy.

"Never mind." Techy laughs and walks out of the room, probably to get out of firing range.

I peek out from behind Liam, and Kyle is standing there with his arms across his chest. "Your secret is safe with me," I tell him.

He winks and walks toward his office.

Liam turns around and looks at me, confused. "What secret?"

I throw my arms up. "I am afraid that I can't tell you." I slip out of his arms and back toward the kitchen. There are butterflies in my stomach just from Liam's touch and the excitement of his birthday.

I can't wait.

Kyle steps into the middle of the room, and I peek over at Tyler, Shane, and Brett, who are standing together drinking beer. Liam is standing next to me, his hand resting on my ass. My dad is across the room with Kayla in front of him, his arms around her. The rest of the guys with ole ladies are in similar positions.

We are a family. The kids are in one of the playrooms with a babysitter Kyle keeps on hand.

Kyle looks at the three prospects, and they stand up straighter under his gaze. "Today is the day we are welcoming some new brothers into the club." I look at the guys and see the utter shock on their faces. They never had the slightest clue what was happening. The earliest someone has ever gotten into the club was after two years as a prospect. Butcher walks over and hands Kyle three cuts. "I know the usual is two years, but you have shown the club that you belong, over and over again. You have earned the respect of everyone in the room."

I smile at their expressions, loving every second of it. I love to see the pure happiness on their faces, and I can tell how much they wanted this.

Vanessa smiles at Tyler, rubbing his back.

"Tyler, come here," Kyle says.

Vanessa takes his beer, and he walks over to Kyle. Kyle has the cut open, and Tyler slides his arms in. The cut has "Devil Souls MC" stitched on it and, under that, "Tyler."

Everyone claps, whistles, and stomps their feet in congratulations. Tyler grins at everyone in the room and hugs Kyle.

"Shane!"

Shane walks over and slips on his cut. His smile is blinding the whole room, and this is probably the first time I have ever seen him smile. He hugs Kyle and walks into the swarm of brothers. Liam is there too; he left me once Tyler got his cut.

Kyle calls, "Brett!"

Brett walks up to Kyle and slips on the cut, his eyes closed and his head back. This means a lot to him. He turns around and hugs Kyle like the others did and, like the others, he is swarmed.

"Welcome to the family!" Kyle says one last time and looks at me, signaling my turn. He walks toward the back of the club.

I walk to the middle of the floor. I smile at everyone in the room, and Liam looks at me, confused. I clap my hands together, winking at Liam. He arches an eyebrow at me.

"So tomorrow is Liam's birthday, and I have a surprise for him." He looks shocked. I hold my hand out, and he walks over and takes it. "Baby, I love you so much. Happy early birthday." I kiss him right in front of the whole club.

The door opens, and Kyle peeks out. I give him a nod, letting him know. He pushes the door open, and in comes the bike that Liam has been wanting for so long, with a nice big red bow on it. His mouth drops open. Braelyn and Ethan walk in behind the bike.

"Paisley, what have you done?" His eyes are on me; then they go back to the bike.

"I found the bike." I smile and he sweeps me up in his arms, kissing me hard.

"Thank you so much, Baby." He sets me down and walks over to the bike, admiring it. I have tears in my eyes at the sight of him being so happy and surprised. I love that I could do this for him. Yeah, he could have bought it for himself, but he could never find one for sale.

I feel someone standing beside me, and I look over and see Dad. "You did good, baby girl." My heart is light and full of happiness.

The door to the kitchen is pushed open, and I see the cake on a rolling table. The candles are already lit. Shaylin starts pushing the cake into the room. "Happy Birthday..." I start the song, and he whips around to see the giant cake. His head shakes in disbelief once more. "Make a wish!" Shaylin tells him.

He never takes his eyes off of me. "I already got my wish."

Oh my god, I could die right this minute. "Baby," I whisper and he bends down and blows out his candles. There are *aww*s all around the room, from all of the ole ladies. This man is going to kill me. I didn't think I could love him any more than I already do, but he does things like this, surprising me.

"I guess I got another surprise myself," he announces. He splits the distance between us and his hands cup my face. "Baby, I love you."

"I love you," I reply, my words breathy.

He lets my face go, his hands dragging down my arms, and he bends down on one knee. Is what I think is happening really happening right now?

"Liam?"

He reaches into his pocket and brings out a box. Yeah, this is really happening! He opens the box, and I gasp at the sight of the beautiful ring. The band is rose gold, and there is a huge diamond with small ones wrapped around it. "Paisley, will you do me the greatest fucking honor and marry me?"

"Yes!" I scream loudly and everyone cheers. Liam slips on the ring and stands up, lifting me off the ground. He kisses me hard, and my legs are wrapped around his waist.

Oh my god! I can't believe this is happening. I am engaged to the man I fell in love with eight years ago, the person who saved me from a horrible fate—god knows what would have happened to me.

The man who was my first kiss.

My first everything, the man I love with all of my heart.

"'I love you so much," I whisper, tears falling down my face. My whole body feels like it's about to burst.

"I love you too, my love."

The room is completely quiet. All of the ladies are crying, and the men are staring at us. We probably look like loons, but he is my loon. I love him so much. He is my life. I couldn't imagine a day without him, and the wait for him was worth every single minute because, in the end, I have him. This is the man I am going to marry, and we are going to have babies and build an amazing family. A family that I will cherish with all of my heart. My kids will grow up being around the best kind of family. The kind that will take care of you, love you unconditionally, and protect you above everything else.

That is family.

That is Liam.

This is my everything.

Liam

She fucking surprised me. I never expected for her to do that for me. She got me the bike I have been searching for forever. She did that for me. Nobody has done anything like that for me, cared that much, or put in that much time and effort. I am so fucking blessed to have her in my life. My fiancé. I bought the ring a long time ago. I have been waiting for the perfect time and I knew, in that moment, that it was time.

I am so surprised by everything she's done. I love that woman with all of my heart. More than life itself. I would do anything for her, and I love her more every day. Call me a pussy or a bitch but I don't care, because I love her. If that makes me a pussy, I will gladly accept that name.

The cartel has been hidden for a long time, but we brought the war to them the moment they perched on club territory and went after Paisley twice. The first time I was there and they never touched her, but the second time they threw fucking acid over the gate. That shit hurt her bad. She was in horrible pain and bedridden for a long time.

She still hasn't gone back to work, and I hope she doesn't because I want her barefoot and pregnant. Plus I am fucking scared of what could happen when she is at work. I can't control what happens to her there.

That shit kills me.

I am not scared of fucking anything, but I am scared of one thing, and that is losing her. The sight of her lying on the ground, not moving and passed out, will forever haunt me. I have nightmares of losing her. I can hardly stand being away from her. That shit is smothering me.

My whole fucking life I just had to worry about myself. Then, when I was seventeen, this blond, blue-eyed angel popped into my life, and it was forever changed.

Fuck me.

She is lying on the couch watching TV in underwear and my shirt. I am standing in the entrance to the living room, just staring at her like a creeper. She looks up and sees me staring at her, and she waves me over. "Come. Cuddle, Baby."

You know what I am going to fucking do? Go cuddle.

Well, maybe not so much fucking cuddling, I have other things in mind.

twelve

Paisley

A Week Later

What the fuck?

In my locker at work there is a letter, and I have no clue how it got there. The letter says: *He is going to pay.* Is this the cartel?

I get a text from Liam letting me know that he is outside. I slam my locker closed and stuff the note in my purse. I will show Liam once I am in the truck.

I keep my eyes peeled, looking for anything and everything out of the ordinary. I am scared; my heart feels like it's about to burst.

Having been burned like that has me on edge constantly. I am scared that something like that will happen again, and I can only relax when I am with Liam. He makes me feel safe and so secure. It's something that I can't describe.

Through the sliding glass doors, I see Liam waiting at the entrance. I let out a deep breath, trying to control myself. I don't want to show my panic just yet. I walk outside, and Liam wraps his arm around me, as usual, hurrying to the truck. He is super happy over his bike, but he doesn't want me on the back of it until everything is settled, and I understand why. It's dangerous.

I just want things to go back to normal. I want to go on bike rides with Liam. I want to go places alone without worrying about something happening. I just want as normal a life as possible, but we all know that's not going to happen.

Liam helps me into the truck and shuts the door. I stick my hand in my purse and take out the note, hating to show it to him because our lives have been quiet and peaceful. Liam stares at me, and I look out the windshield. "Baby?"

I close my eyes, hearing the concern in his voice, and my stomach twists. The cartel has gone after me twice; why the fuck are they doing it again? What do they want with me?

I hand the note to Liam and watch his expression as he reads it. Just as I expected, he is extremely pissed off. He starts the truck, and his hands clutch the steering wheel tightly. The veins in his arms are straining from the exertion, and his jaw is clenching and unclenching.

"Let's go home, I will call the guys over." He takes my hand and kisses the back of it. I scoot toward him, close my eyes, and lie on his shoulder. Everything will be okay. This will all end someday—it can't last forever.

It can't.

I am drained; I am so tired of all this stuff. It's been going on for months, and as soon as we get a break, they start up their shit again.

"It's okay, sweet girl, but I don't think it's safe for you to go back to work unless you let me put someone on you."

I want to work—being a nurse is what I have wanted for so long—but if it means endangering my life or someone else's, its best to take some vacation time. "I will call tomorrow and let them know." I can hear the sadness in my voice. I hate that they are taking this away from me.

"I am sorry, Baby, but I can't risk something happening to you," he whispers.

I squeeze his hand tighter. "I understand, Baby." We sit in silence for a few minutes, thinking of all the shit that has gone down. I notice a beat-up old van on my side of the vehicle. I sit up higher in my seat. I have a bad feeling.

The driver's window slowly moves down, and the barrel of a gun sticks out. I grip Liam's leg. "Liam!" I yell. He looks over as a shot goes off, the sound loud and thunderous. The bullet hits the window but doesn't pierce it.

Thank God every vehicle we get the for the club adds a lot of safety features. The moment a bullet hits the window, the club is notified. Liam pushes me onto the floor and puts a bulletproof vest between the door and me.

"I am going straight to the club." He floors it. "Let's hope this fucker follows us right to the club. I am going to make them fucking pay." He lets off the gas for a second as we swerve through town.

I lie on the floor, while god knows what is happening above me, but I am not scared. That probably isn't a normal reaction at all, but I grew up with this life. I know that Liam will protect me. Even with all of this going on, I wouldn't change a thing. This is my life.

A few bursts of gunfire hit the back of the truck, and I hear the ping of the bullets bouncing off. I wince. It's going to be hard to get the bullets out of his new truck.

"I am going to fucking kill them," Liam says.

Then I hear the amazing sound of bikes. The club has come to us. I look out the back window; the van comes to a dead stop in the midst of all the traffic and pulls into an alley.

"Liam, they are going to get away," I inform him, sitting up in my seat.

"Baby, I'd rather you be safe. Fuck that fucker. You're more important and I am not leaving you alone."

Be still my heart, he is so fucking beautiful and has the best heart. The bikes have surrounded us. My father is right outside my window, and I wave at him. He shakes his head, smiling, and waves back, and we are escorted back to the club. The gate slams behind us and Liam pulls me into the driver's seat and pulls me out of the truck with him.. Everyone climbs off his bike, and my father runs over.

"I am fine, Dad!" I reassure him.

He lets out a deep breath but still looks concerned.

"What the fuck happened, Liam?" Kyle asks.

Liam hands over the note. "Paisley found this in her locker at work, and then when we were driving home someone shot at us, in an old fucking van."

Kyle reads the note out loud, as Liam rubs my back soothingly. I gnaw on my bottom lip, expecting the van to pop up any second.

"You okay, baby girl?" A hand touches my arm. Dad is standing in front of me, still looking concerned.

"I'm okay, Daddy." I smile.

He studies my face and I don't think he believes me.

I'm just exhausted and disappointed that they are taking my work away, but if it weren't for us, the entire town would be swarmed. This place is safer than most cities, because the MC controls the drugs and other horrible things coming through. This town means a lot to us. I grew up here, and I plan to raise my kids here. I want them to have the childhood I had, which is why this cartel needs to go.

I hear squealing tires, and I look through the gate just as that same van approaches. Its window is down and a gun is pointing right at me. I gasp loudly, frozen in my place.

Liam

In a split second I have my arm around her waist, lifting her and putting her in the truck as the gunshots go off.

I turn around and face the shooter. The shooter is hitting the gate, which is fucking bulletproof, but not piercing it. I walk straight toward him, opening my arms wide with a fucking smile on my face. The bullets hit the gate right in front of my face. I bring both of my middle fingers up.

The bullets stop, and all I can see is a crack in one of the tinted windows. My brothers are at my back.

"What the fuck do you want?" I yell, and the vehicle just fucking takes off.

"Just let it go." Kyle puts his hand on my chest, stopping me from running to my bike.

"This person is trying to hurt her." I am pissed off that Kyle is trying to stop me from doing what needs to be done to eliminate the problem.

Kyle looks me dead in the fucking face. "Liam, I don't fucking think this is the cartel." I think back to all of the details, the shitty van and the note that says that I am going to pay. Holy fuck.

"Fuck me, I don't know who it could be, Kyle." I don't know what to fucking think; this shit is unreal. I don't have any enemies besides the enemies of the MC.

Kyle looks out the gate, where the van was. "Just keep your eyes peeled, Liam."

What the fuck is happening? Why the fuck are they going for Paisley if they have a problem with me?

Paisley

Liam is stone-faced and filled with anger. He'd better not be blaming himself for this stuff.

Shane helps me out of Liam's truck, and I walk over to him. I put my hands on his chest to get his attention, and he acts like I am not even here. He is still staring at the same spot.

"Baby?" I reach up, putting my hands on either side of his face, and force him to turn and look at me.

He finally looks at me, and I know that he is trying to control his anger. He doesn't like me to see that side of him.

"Baby, don't," I warn him.

A little smile tugs at his lips.

"Come on, give me some sugar," I tease him, my lips pooched out for a kiss. He rolls his eyes and kisses me. I close my eyes, all joking gone the moment his lips touch mine.

"Not in front of me," Dad growls behind me, and I laugh against Liam's lips and pull away.

Kyle looks at both of us, smiling. "Why don't you guys go home, and I will put Techy on this."

Liam nods and Dad takes my hand and pulls me to him. My heart hurts at the scared look on his face. I have only seen that look on his face a time or two, and that was when Kayla was in danger.

"Dad, I am fine," I whisper, tugging on his vest. He pulls me to him, and I lay my head on his chest.

"It's fucking killing me people are trying to hurt you, baby girl. I want to tuck you away and hide you. Liam would fucking kill me if I tried."

"Damn right," Liam says.

I laugh loudly, because Liam doesn't give a fuck what my dad thinks, and he sure isn't scared of him. My dad is huge, tattooed, and scarred; he is not someone people would mess with. Even when he was seventeen years old, Liam would sneak in my window, and Dad never found out. Even if he had, Liam probably would have just smiled through it all.

"You've had her enough, give her back." Liam grabs the back of my pants, pulling me away from Dad. I laugh again, as Dad grabs my hands and it's like a tug of war. "Come on, you guys," I manage to get out through my laughter, my stomach already hurting. Dad finally lets me go with a pretend huff, and Liam pulls me back to his side.

"I love you guys."

Dad smiles. "I love you too, baby girl."

Liam kisses my temple. "I love you too, my love."

thirteen

Paisley

Two Days Later

I wake up to the feel of Liam between my legs. "Liam," I whisper, my voice deep, smoky from sleep. He burrows his head deeper, sucking my clit farther into his mouth, and my toes curl instantly. That is the thing that drives me crazy more than anything.

"Just fuck me." My whole body is begging for it. He shakes his head, which causes his teeth to pull my clit.

"FUCK!" I scream, my legs shaking hard. He chuckles, his fingers digging into the outside of my thighs. "Baby, please, I beg you." Liam raises his head, stares at me, and crawls up my body, giving in. I feel him right at the entrance, and I bend my hips, trying to slide him inside me. "Please," I beg.

His hand strokes my cheek, his thumb moving over my lips. "Please what?" The hand moves down to my breast, the same thumb stroking my nipple.

"I want you, Baby."

His hand strokes my side. I shiver at the contact, goose bumps breaking out across my skin. "Then my Baby can have me," he whispers and my whole body shivers at his words. He pushes inside, all the way to the hilt.

My head falls back, exposing my throat, and he kisses my throat while moving inside me, slowly and so sexily.

"God, Baby, I love you." I put my legs around his waist.

He looks into my eyes, his elbows by my face, his movements slow, making love to me.

Liam and I fuck a lot, multiple times a day, honestly, but these are the moments I treasure more than anything. We connect on a different level when we slow things down and just *feel*. We feel the love that we share.

I love him so much.

I drag my fingernails up and down his back lightly. "My Liam," I whisper, my back arching when he hits that special spot.

"My love." He bends his head and kisses me softly. "Now I fuck you," he growls, and he hammers into me hard and relentlessly. I enjoy every single second of it.

I hold onto him and hang on for the ride, and what a fucking ride it is.

Liam is outside doing something. I left a note on the table: *Come find me, Baby.*

I left him a Nerf gun on the table, and now I am sitting at the top of the stairs, lying down on my stomach so he doesn't see me, waiting for him to come in. Once reads the note I am going to get him. Through the window I see him on the front porch.

Almost show time.

He comes in, takes his shoes off, and shuts the door, and he looks up and sees the note. I bite my lip trying to hide my laughter as he reads it and looks at the Nerf gun. I sit up and press my gun through the stair railings, pointing it directly at him. I pull the trigger, the foam Nerf bullet hits him on the chest, and his head shoots up. He looks at me with an evil grin on his face.

Oh fuck.

I get up and run to the back stairway. I can hear him running behind me, and if I don't do something quickly he is going to find me easily. I turn around and see that he is coming fast. I aim my gun and pull the trigger, hitting him right in the chest. He lifts his gun and hits me right on the ass—how original—and he does this again and again.

"Hey!" I yell and stop running. I turn around to face him, and another bullet hits me on the tit. He pulls the trigger again and hits my other tit.

"Baby," I scold and he laughs hard. He throws down his gun and grabs me so quickly that I didn't have a chance to move. "Baby, we have to go to the club. All of the women are practicing shooting." He laughs at my pouting, and he bends down and throws me over his shoulder.

"Let me down, Liam!" I yell with mock anger.

He laughs again, his hand landing hard on my ass. I jolt from the small sting. "Hey!" I yell and reach down, grabbing his ass. He carries me right out of the house and straight to his truck, which is now fixed. The club owns a few body shops, so it was no problem getting it fixed so soon.

The MC has their fingers in a lot of things; we have a car dealership and everything. It's wild to see everything we own. My dad and Kyle were the founders; they started the clubs from nothing. They wanted the club to be a family; they wanted to make sure that their kids and generations to come would never have to worry about money. They wanted to keep everyone safe and secure.

My dad was never in the military; he was a single father at nineteen years old and he raised me. He raised me by himself for years until he met Kyle—and Kyle, along with the other guys, helped him out. Dad took me bra shopping and that was the most uncomfortable thing in the whole world, trying to find the kind of bra I needed. He acted like it was the most normal thing in the world, but I know he was screaming and cussing on the inside.

I am glad that he has Kayla. They have the kind of love that everyone strives to have, and I have that with Liam. I wake up in the middle of the night and think, how did I get so lucky and blessed? I thank God every single day for him.

These past two days Liam and I have barely made it out of bed. We stayed in and vegged in front of the TV. Today we got the call from Kyle at our gun range that they want us women to learn to shoot. Luckily for me I know how to shoot.

We pull up outside the gun range. "You going to teach me how to shoot?" I ask Liam, acting all innocent. I don't think he knows that I know how to shoot; he definitely doesn't know how good I am at it. Dad has had me shooting since I was old enough to learn how to do it safely. He carries a gun everywhere, so it was only fitting that I learn about gun safety.

"Sure, Baby." He leans across the middle seat and kisses me. He gets out of the truck, and I let a laugh loose because he is about to get the shock of his life.

I get out of the truck and walk to where the ole ladies are standing. Liam is getting his guns out of his truck.

"You girls ready?" Kyle calls, and Liam walks over and sets stuff down on the table.

Liam grabs a small pistol. "I am going to show Paisley how to shoot really fast before we start," he tells Kyle, and my dad looks at me, confused.

I wink at him, and he covers his mouth to hide his smile. Kyle looks just as confused since he taught me, right along with my dad. I put my finger up to my mouth.

Liam has me stand in front of a target and shows me the ropes, explaining everything. "Alright baby, step back here and do exactly as I told you."

I walk back to where he told me to stand, pretending I still don't have a clue what I am doing. I adjust my stance as he instructed me to do; it's really the same thing I was taught all those years ago.

"Shoot whenever you are ready, Baby." Liam's hand is on the small of my back, bracing me.

I aim and pull the trigger.

Liam

I think I have been played. I realized it the moment she pulled the trigger and the bullet hit the fucking bull's eye.

She empties the clip and then Torch is there, handing her a fucking AK. She takes the gun like a fucking pro and shoots every single target, hitting the dummies right between the fucking eyes and on the heart.

All of a sudden Torch and Kyle are standing beside me.

"She fucking played me," I say.

They laugh loudly. "Fuck yeah, she did, we both taught her."

She empties the clip once again and turns around, looking at me with a shit-eating grin on her face.

Little fucker.

She walks over to me, hands her dad the fucking gun, and continues giving me that grin. "Thanks for all your help, Baby."

I glare at her, everyone behind me laughing. I am pretty sure Torch is about to roll on the fucking ground he is so amused. I bend down and whisper in her ear, "You're going to get it later."

She pulls back, grinning at me even wider now. "Promise?"

I nod. Her dad isn't fucking smiling now, and that serves him right. She walks back to the ole ladies; even Vanessa is there.

Paisley

He is so shocked!" Kayla laughs loudly. Honestly, he was. I got him good and I have the promise of payback later, and I can't wait. Payback isn't really payback with Liam because I benefit from it, and I may or may not piss him off on purpose. My dad and Kyle ate that shit up. They loved to see me play a prank on Liam, especially since they taught me everything I know.

"I am excited to learn!" Vanessa says, watching the guys preparing the guns. I feel like this is a big deal for her; this will give her a way to protect herself. I want that for her. She has suffered at the hands of other people without a way to protect herself, and this will give her that independence.

I have my carry and conceal license, and I keep my gun in my car. I drive home a lot at night, and there are some messed-up people in this world.

"I am so shocked that you can shoot that good, girl!" Vanessa tells me, a huge grin on her face, and I am taken aback for a second. She looks different. She looks happy, like the weight of the world has been lifted off her shoulders and, honestly, it is probably because of her dad. He probably had her so down all of the time. Since she has been with Tyler, she is so much happier. I love to see her this way, and I want her to grow and have all the things she has been missing in life.

"How are things with you and Tyler?" I ask her.

She smiles even bigger, and she looks over her shoulder at him and then back at me. He is standing next to Liam, talking. "Things are amazing, girl, I am so glad that you set us up. I am so happy now, girl, and sometimes I am afraid that something could take that away any minute." She looks down at the ground, her fingers twisting the bottom of her shirt.

I touch her arm. "You can't think like that, girl, you need to live and enjoy every moment."

She smiles softly. "I just love him."

I smile back. "I know exactly how you feel." Liam catches me looking at him, winking across the yard.

A few hours later, we are eating lunch at one of the many restaurants the MCs own in town. This is the first time we have all gotten together like this in a while. The cartel hitting us changed a lot of things in our MC, and it changed the Grim Sinners also. They have been fighting the same battle.

I love seeing the smiling and happy faces of my family. All the kids are at the clubhouse; it's the safest place at the moment. We have Shane, Brett, and a couple of nannies watching them, and the place is completely locked down via Techy.

A hand touches my inner thigh and, from the corner of my eye, I see Liam smirking. He wants to play?

We will see about that.

I reach under the table, making sure that I don't bump his hand. I smile to myself and grab his dick. He jumps so hard that his knees hit the table, and everyone turns to look at him, confused. What do I do? I keep on rubbing. A strong hand wraps around my wrist and pulls my hand away. I bite my bottom lip, hiding my laughter. I look at Liam like I just don't know what happened.

Everyone goes back to their conversations and their food. Liam leans toward me, and I feel his breath on my ear. "Payback, Baby," he whispers. He doesn't scare me—that's for sure— because I reap the benefits of his threats. His payback means orgasms.

"Is everyone ready to go?" Kyle asks.

Everyone gets up and files to the door and, as if in one motion, the girls are put in the middle, between all the guys.

We all walk outside, and I'm holding Liam's hand. Alisha is on the other side, holding Techy's hand, and she smiles at me. Alisha has been an amazing friend over the years. She is close to me in age. She was around twenty when she and Techy got together; he is a couple of years older.

She had a very rough childhood. Techy literally took her out of her fucked-up situation and gave her the life she deserves. She wanted to be a mother more than anything else, and she is doing exactly that, while her man worships the ground she walks on.

"Baby, do you want to order takeout?" I stop at the sight of a black SUV speeding by, the window rolled down. Liam presses my head into his chest then falls to the ground, breaking my fall with his free arm as bullets ring out around us, hitting vehicles. I look out from under Liam's arm to see all the other ladies are covered the same way. Alisha has her eyes closed and her face in the crook of Techy's neck. Dad is staring down at Kayla, his mouth moving to reassure her. I can see the slight panic on her face.

The bullets stop a few seconds later, and I hear the squeal of the vehicle driving off, then silence. I don't hear anything but the sound of Liam breathing above me. "Baby?" I whisper. His hand cups my face, letting me know he hears me, before he looks up at everyone.

"Everyone okay?" Kyle asks.

I relax at the sound of everyone's voices telling him they are okay. This was the cartel. I knew it the moment I saw the vehicle.

"We need to make a run and go to the vehicles. I don't like being a sitting duck," Kyle says. I can almost feel the anger radiating off of him.

"One, two, three. GO!" he yells and I am swept off the ground. Liam has me tucked against his chest, running with me.

My heart stops at the sound of gunshots hitting close to me and Liam. He runs faster and I hear his truck door open. He climbs into the passenger side with me in his lap. The door shuts and I can breathe. I look out the window, frantically checking on my family.

One by one they get in their vehicles. Bullets are hitting the windows but not piercing the glass. Thank God for the club updating the vehicles. Kyle's vehicle is parked right next to ours, and he looks so fucking pissed off. He picks up his phone, and I hear Liam's phone vibrating.

Liam takes it out. "We are heading to the back-up club. The kids are at the other one." He scoots across to his seat.

Kyle drives out of the parking lot, not stopping even though the bullets are nailing his truck. We are the next to go, but I am not playing fucking games. I reach in the backseat and grab my AK. I roll down the window enough to shoot out of it; then I nail the fucking vehicle. I shoot out the passenger window and hit the gunman on the fucking arm.

Liam laughs loudly then puts the truck in park and scoots to the middle of the seat. He takes aim and hits the driver. I keep firing my AK, destroying the vehicle. Then I shoot the front of the vehicle, blowing the fucker up.

I hear a lot of yelling and whistles. I roll down my window and stick my head out, smiling at everyone and holding up my AK. The old me wouldn't have done that, but I can't stand the thought of my family getting hurt so I took it into my own hands and did what I thought was needed. I took them out.

Kyle has backed into the parking lot. "Let's go to the clubhouse then." He laughs and takes off again.

On the way back to the clubhouse, I notice another SUV and I know that this is another cartel vehicle. Rolling down my window halfway, I lift out my AK one more time and destroy their vehicle then lift my middle finger.

The women are not to be fucked with. I am tired of this shit, and I am not going to take it anymore. Ole ladies are not people to fucking mess with. I am tired of them messing with my family. It's time that I fight back, and that's what I am going to do and give them a taste of their own medicine.

Game on.

fourteen

Paisley

A Few Days Later

The other ladies and I have decided to have a girls' shopping day. It's the first time we've done this in months because of everything that has been going down, and it's much needed. I am also running out of underwear because Liam has a huge habit of tearing them off my body. We fuck a couple of times a day, and it seems that neither Liam nor I can get enough.

"This day was much needed!" Chrystal says and plops down in the chair next to me in one of the restaurants in the mall. From the corner of my eye, I see a man who looks like Liam. But when I look back he is gone, so I don't say anything.

I nod, taking a drink of my water. "I needed this so bad, I needed some normal."

The girls around me pipe up in agreement. We are not alone. Members of the MC are sitting all around us, at different tables, keeping an eye on us—but they are doing their own thing.

Liam is sitting two tables over, not bothering to pretend that he's not keeping an eye on me. Everything that has been going on has him seriously on edge. I don't blame him because, honestly, I am the exact same way.

Liam winks at me and finally looks away. As I turn back to the girls, I see a man ducking into the men's bathroom. I could swear it's the same man I saw earlier, the guy who looks like Liam. Eating my food I watch for the man to come back out, but he doesn't. Why do I have a bad feeling?

Everyone parts ways as we finish eating. It's safer if we don't leave at once; traveling as a group puts a bigger target on our backs.

Liam and I are heading home to stay in bed for the rest of the day, watching TV and fucking. I can't wait for the moment that all of this ends so I can marry him and have babies. I want at least two: a little boy who looks just like Liam and a sweet little angel. I know that Liam would be an amazing father. He had such a shitty childhood and he said, years ago, that if he became a father he would do everything in his power to be the best, and I believe him.

Liam has his hand pressed on the small of my back, and his head is swiveling in every direction, looking for any kind of danger.

"Do you want take—" I don't finish. Hands are buried in my hair and I am pulled back hard, right out of Liam's arms and onto the ground. The air is knocked out of my lungs. Someone is holding my throat—I cannot breathe. Liam is fighting six men all at once. Oh my god, we are being attacked.

Liam takes a hit to the face. He stops moving and wipes the blood off his lip and smiles. Oh fuck. He rolls his shoulder and then he explodes. I push myself up, ignoring the stinging on my bare arms and legs from fucking road burn, my head hurting like a bitch.

Another guy is running toward us, coming straight for me. I push myself up to a standing position, ready to fight. The guy reaches me, and I aim a kick straight for his nuts. He dodges and bends down, throwing me over his shoulder. I beat his back, pulling his grimy hair hard, and then he is running with me. I twist, pull, and hit with everything in me.

I look up and see Liam knocking out the last man. I scream and he looks at me in pure horror. He takes off after us, and I am thrown in the van and the door is slammed shut behind me.

It hits me like a ton of bricks: I have been kidnapped. I spin around and face whoever is in the van with me. I am face-to-face with the man I saw at the mall, the one who looks like Liam.

"What do you want?" I ask him. My voice is completely calm but, on the inside, I am anything but that. I am scared.

"I have a message for Liam." The guy smiles, his teeth dirty. His whole face is dirty with god knows what, and his hair hasn't been in a shower in a very long time.

I don't say a word. I just want to hear what he has to say. "Tell Liam that I can take everything away from him just like he did me."

The doors are opened behind me, and I see Liam. My captor is gone. Then I am pushed out of the van, right onto the highway.

Liam

"FUCK!" I yell at the sight of her hitting the fucking ground. I was going to take every one of them at the next red light, but they came to an almost-stop and threw her out. I put the car in park and run over to her. My hands are a fucking mess bleeding and cracked and my face is bleeding. I took on six fucking men who all wanted to fight at one time.

She is sitting up when I reach her. She lifts her arms, and I lift her off the ground and run back to my truck so I can get her out of the open. She sits in the middle of the seat, staring through the windshield, and her arms are messed up because of road burn.

"Baby." I touch her face, not even caring that I have traffic backed up.

"He had a message for you, he wanted you to know that he can take everything away from you like you did him."

What the living fuck is going on? I have not taken anything from anyone. I have been overseas for fucking years. I put the truck in drive and race for the fucking clubhouse, hitting the fucking alert button on the roof of my truck, letting them all know that shit is going down.

Paisley is curled into my side, her whole body shaking, and I fucking hate it. I hate that I wasn't there to protect her. I fought off six fucking guys at once, and I thought she was hiding. Then I heard her scream, and the fucker tossed her into the vehicle. I never had a fucking chance to get to her.

"Don't do that, Liam." Paisley says, rubbing my chest. "Don't blame yourself."

It's hard not to, when something like that happens right under my fucking nose, and who the fuck is this person? Is it someone I have tortured over the years? Did I kill someone they are close to?

I don't fucking know!

I pull through the gate and vehicles pull in behind us. I look in the mirror and see my face is red with blood. One of the fuckers had steel knuckles, and it got me on the forehead. Paisley is unhurt besides her road burn.

I open my door and step out, and I reach in and pick Paisley up. Everyone surrounds us. It's like a fucking dream; why the fuck are they going for her? I explain what happened, and I carry her inside the clubhouse. Guilt is eating me alive, because this is happening because of me.

Paisley

I can tell that guilt is eating him alive, but I won't allow him to feel that way if I can help it. The person who attacked us is obviously crazy.

Myra, another ole lady, is cleaning my road burn. Liam should have been treated first because of his head wound, but he wouldn't have it. He is glued to my side.

Kyle walks into the room and throws Liam a pair of keys. "Go to the mountains and hide out, the caretaker is stocking everything as we speak. We are going to find this fucker. In the meantime, you guys need peace."

Myra finishes with me and goes to Liam. The cut isn't that bad, but head wounds always bleed the worst. I grip Liam's hand, and hope blooms in my chest for the first time in a while.

I can't wait to get away from everything and just relax.

If only it were that simple.

fifteen

Paisley

We got to the cabin a few hours ago. I am sitting on the edge of the bed with Liam on his knees in front of me, his head in my lap. My hand is running gently through his hair and down his back. His body softens, under my hands, for the first time in a long time.

It seems like, even in sleep, his whole body is hard and waiting for anything. I think being in this house in the middle of nowhere, under a different name, we cannot be found.

"You okay, Liam?" I whisper. I bend down and kiss the back of his head. His hand tightens around my hip, just holding me.

"I am fine, Baby." He sighs loudly, his head burrowing between my legs, and I laugh because his nose is right at my crotch now.

"Baby." I laugh and he laughs right along with me.

He shakes his head once again, and I open my legs, laughing even harder. Liam raises his head, smiling for the first time since everything happened.

I reach out and touch the side of his face. "Now that is my Liam."

His face softens, smiling at me sweetly.

"I love you, Liam."

His hand rests on my cheek and mine on his, before his forehead leans against mine. "I love you too, my baby."

I know I will never tire of hearing those words. Every single time I hear them, I get butterflies. I know, deep down in my heart, that God has made him for me. Liam is meant to be mine. He is my whole heart, and I pray that everyone finds the kind of love I have. I wish everyone had this happiness; maybe the world would be a better place.

"Baby, I want to fuck you but I think I need to sleep and I want you to hold me."

He nods and gets off the floor, and he strips down. I could fuck Liam twenty-four and seven, but I just want to sleep and feel safe. Liam is the kind of guy who radiates protectiveness and safety. I know that he would do anything to protect me and, even today, I knew he was coming for me. He was right behind the van and I knew, the moment we stopped, he was going to get me.

I pull the comforter back, sliding down the sheets, and close my eyes, relaxing. My body sinks into the bed, which rubs against my road rash, making me hurt.

"You in pain, Baby?" Liam asks me. I crack open one eye only to see him stark naked, and his dick is pointing in my direction.

"I am just a little sore, today has been a crazy day."

Liam looks down at the ground for a few seconds, and I hate that he feels this way. I shouldn't have said anything. I don't want him to feel any guilt at all. "Baby, don't you fucking dare blame yourself!" I tell him once again, and he looks at me and rolls his eyes.

My mouth opens in shock that he would roll his eyes at me. "You didn't just do that," I hiss, pretending to be mad, wanting to draw him out of this mood. I turn onto my stomach and lie with my head on the pillow, and he crawls into bed with me and smacks me on the ass.

I laugh and scoot over to lie on his chest. The heat radiates off of him immediately, making my day so much better, and I feel safety coming off of him in waves.

"It just fucking scares me the thought of something happening to you," he whispers and turns off the light, bringing us into complete darkness.

I run my hand down his side. "Baby, I love you so much and I knew you were coming for me, but you're not Superman. You're the only man I know who could take on six men at once with barely a scratch."

His head tilts to the side and he kisses my forehead. "Still doesn't make it easier on me, Baby." His fingers are buried in my hair, which is sore from the hair pulling I got earlier, soothing me.

"Baby, I can't stand you being hurt, it fucking kills me on the inside. It goes against everything in me for you to be in danger, it's against my very core."

Tears pool behind my eyelids and I try not to cry. When you love someone it's so hard to think about them being hurt, and I hate the thought of Liam in danger. I wanted to help him so badly today, but I learned a long time ago to let him handle it, rather than distracting him and making it worse.

"You know I can't wait for the day we are living in peace. We can get married and have a bunch of babies," I pipe in, wanting to break the mood.

He bursts out laughing, kissing the side of my head once more. "I will have to fucking hide for a year because your dad will try to kill me."

I laugh loudly at that because he is not lying. My father never took to me dating in the first place, and he gave Liam a hard time. Liam made it worse on himself because he

never gave a fuck if my father harassed him. He would laugh, which pissed my dad off worse.

I also know that, deep down, Dad actually likes him. Dad bought Liam his first bike when he was seventeen and pretended it was a club thing. Liam saved me. He saved me from something that would have forever affected my life, if I'd survived. I could have killed, or god knows what else could have happened to me. I might never have been found. If it weren't for Liam, everything would be so different. My life wouldn't be my life. Liam is my life, and he has been since I was sixteen years old.

"You know Dad never found out that you used to sneak in my window almost every night."

Liam laughs. "Well, I would probably be dead because your dad would have shot my ass for sneaking in his daughter's window."

I agree. "Well, I loved the thrill of it."

"I bet you did, mean ass." He smacks my ass once more and continues cupping my ass cheek.

"I loved every moment I had with you, especially right before you left. I missed you so much, and I counted down the days until you were home."

He holds me a little tighter. "Baby, you're the one thing that kept me going while I was over there. With the shit I've seen and done... It was you who made me go to sleep smiling because it would all be fucking worth it in the end, because I would have you." He stops for a few beats, pulling me even closer. "Over the years I would come home, and I would see the changes in you, you turning into the most beautiful woman."

He pushes me onto my back and looks down at me. "When I first met you, I made a promise to myself that I would make myself worthy of you. I knew that I never would be, but I vowed I would never fucking give you up."

He kisses my forehead before letting his head rest against mine. "You're my Paisley."

I put my hands on either side of his face. "You're my Liam."

He closes his eyes. I do the same, just feeling him and enjoying the amazing feeling of loving him and him loving me back. It's the best feeling in the world.

The Next Morning

Liam and I are cooking breakfast together. The windows are open, letting in the early morning breeze, and we're enjoying the peace. A song comes on the radio, "You Make It Easy" by Jason Aldean. Hands are on my waist. I turn around and he pulls me into his arms. I lay my head on his chest, hands on his ass, eyes closed, and he sways us side to side listening to the words.

God, I love him so much.

I open my eyes, looking up at him, and he smiles and touches my cheek. "I have something for you." I leave him standing in the middle of the kitchen, and I run upstairs to my suitcase and pull out the journal.

This journal is my journey with Liam: the moment I first saw him, when he saved me, and over the years. I want him to know how I feel, and my talking about my feelings will never be enough.

I walk back to the kitchen. Liam is leaning against the counter, and I hand him the journal. "This is for you."

He studies the back of the journal and looks at me, confused. "This is our journey, in my eyes, from the moment I first saw you until the moment we were engaged." He eyes me and then walks into the living room, taking the journal. I let out a deep breath. I'm nervous about seeing his reaction.

Liam

I open the journal not knowing what to expect. I never expected for her to have this journal, and it means a lot that she would go through the trouble of writing all of this down.

Entry Number One:
Today, I saw him for the first time. He is the new kid in school and he has to be the most beautiful man I ever saw. He smiled at me at lunch, and I thought my heart was going to stop in my chest right then and there. My friends were jealous that he even looked at me, but I don't care. I want to marry him. I want him and he is the only boy that I ever thought about liking. The rest are too scared of my father and the club, but I have a feeling he would not care. He is a bad boy and maybe, all along, I have had a thing for them? But I think it's just him.

I laugh out loud at her calling me a bad boy and loving it when I just smiled at her. I remember that moment, because I was so fucking infatuated with her.

Entry Number Two:
He has been staring at me all day. With every single move I make, I can feel his eyes on me. I love that he is staring at me because that means he isn't staring at other girls.

I laugh out loud again because she is right. I could barely take my eyes off her, and I thought I came across as creepy—but, apparently, she liked that shit.

Entry Number Three:
I wish he would talk to me. I wish I had the guts to talk to him.

I so wanted to fucking talk to her. She was so innocent and sweet, I didn't want to taint her with all of my shit. She skipped a few days.

Entry Number Four:
He saved me, he stopped the most horrible thing from happening to me, and I am not sure how I can go on. I am scared that someone could almost do something like this to me so easily—a janitor, no less.
I feel dirty and embarrassed, my stomach is in knots and I am so sick to my stomach. I can feel his hands on me and hear him telling me what is going to happen to me. I was going to be trafficked out. I know that my dad would have done everything in his power to save me, but the damage would have been done. Without Liam I would be gone and probably wishing I were dead.
Liam saved me, but I am not sure that he will ever talk to me again, because who would?

She just fucking broke my heart. It is shattered into a million pieces by knowing that the thought of my not wanting her crossed her mind. That shit is unacceptable. No matter what happened to her, it would never change the way I feel about her.

Entry Number Five:

I thought today was going to end up being a total disaster, my friends completely abandoned me and I was left alone all day at school.

Until lunchtime.

Liam sat down right beside me, and he opened my food and drinks like he has known me for a long time. Then we just hit it off, it ended up being the best day because he was there and, most of all, I felt safe.

I had been scared all day long. People stared, guys leered, and people laughed at me like it was my fault. He made it okay. Today he become a big part of me and he doesn't know it.

Entry Number Six:

He sneaked in my window, my stomach was in knots and my heart felt like it was about to explode. My whole body was on edge, and I was aware of his every move, even though we just watched TV the whole night. I couldn't keep the smile off of my face even if I tried. He wanted to make sure I was okay and didn't want me to be alone.

He wanted to make sure that I was okay.

I know, in this moment, that I could fall in love with him very easily.

There is an entry for every time we did something together or something monumental happened. It could be the littlest thing, like my holding her hand. It meant the fucking world to her, and that shit means everything to me. Because it meant everything to me too. I loved getting to share all of the little things with her. She was the reason I got through being overseas. She helped me heal from a lot of things. My shit childhood made me angry and hateful. But I could never be those things with her; she is Paisley. She changed me.

The entries go on and on: our first time holding hands, the first time we kissed, when we hugged for the first time, and when she rode on the back of my bike. Everything. The moment I left for basic and it was killing her on the inside. She wanted to support me in all of my fucking dreams, but she missed me so much that she felt like she couldn't breathe. I couldn't breathe either, she is my fucking air. I breathe her, she is my whole fucking being.

Then the entries end the moment I got back, the moment I was home with her for fucking good.

I stand up, putting the notebook on the coffee table, and go to find her. She is lying on the bed with another journal, watching TV. She looks up at me with that fucking blinding smile. "Finished?"

What the fuck do I say to that? "Is that another one for me?"

She nods again with the same huge fucking smile. She is so fucking beautiful. I still know that I don't deserve her, but nobody could love her like I do. She closes the book and sets it on the table. "You going to fuck me or what?" She grins.

Paisley

The moment he walks into the room, I can tell that he is looking at me in another light, and that is exactly what my intention was. I wanted him to see the core of my being. I wanted him to see all of me.

There will be more journals for him. I have one for the night of our wedding, and it starts with the moment he came home; that was the beginning of us. Then after we are married, I will start another one, and this will be given to him before we have our first child. I will give him another journal at every huge milestone in our life. I never want him to doubt how I feel.

Liam had such a hard childhood. He was never loved or shown affection, and this is my way of letting him look back, read my words and know that, from the very beginning, I was his. He was my first everything. He was the first guy that I ever held hands with. He was the first person I ever rode on the back of a bike with who wasn't family. He was my first kiss and the first and only person I had sex with. He has all of me and I have all of him. Our first time together was something special because we have only been with each other, and neither of us has ever loved anyone else.

Call me sappy, but I don't care. When you love someone, everything that happens is huge. I am not childish. Everything is just a huge deal because these little things led us here.

Now we fuck. We fuck hard and make love. We are dirty, and I love every single moment of it.

"Paisley?"

I look at Liam, coming out of my daydream.

"Yeah?" I ask him, smirking because he is now naked.

He smirks right back at me. "You better hang on."

Oh boy.

sixteen

Paisley

I wake up to the sound of a siren going off in the house, and I sit up in bed, holding my chest due to having been startled awake. Liam is already out of bed, slipping on clothes, and I do the same. I don't know what is happening.

Liam walks across the bedroom to the TV and turns it on, switching to camera mode. My heart hits the floor at the sight of so many cartel members. Liam looks at me, and I hurry and slip on good shoes and a jacket because it's cold out. Liam runs to the closet and begins taking out guns, and I run over to my phone and hit the panic button. Liam comes out of the closet with AKs, and he hands one to me with a bunch of clips. He carries the other AK with a couple of pistols.

I have a very bad feeling. We are in the middle of nowhere, and the MC is an hour away. We are fucked.

"Baby, we are going to have to run for the mountains," he tells me and I nod. He grabs a backpack, and my guess is that it has supplies.

I look at the monitors, and the intruders are much closer. I know they are cartel because of the distinctive tattoo running up each man's neck. I guess they are still gunning for the women of the club, but Liam and I have been exposed.

"Liam, they must have a tracker on us, or they've followed us," I whisper.

He looks at me and freezes. He grabs my hand, leading me to a small hidden room, and we duck inside. As we crawl through, Liam is pushing the backpacks in front of him and I am carrying my gun.

A few minutes later we come out of the house and are next to the woods. At moments like these, I am so glad that the MC put a lot of work into making sure we have these escape hatches. The house is completely surrounded, and men are standing outside our bedroom window.

Liam grabs my hand and we duck into the woods, running. I hear someone yelling from the house and I know, in that instant, we left the surveillance on and they can see us running. Liam tightens his hand on mine, and we run faster. My lungs are already screaming at me because I am not the most athletic person. My heart is pounding with fear and exertion. My skin is on edge, and it's so cold I can see my breath.

Liam is studying everything around him. I can tell his training has taken over. My hand is shaking in his, more from the cold than being scared. I am scared, but I don't think it's sunk in that there is a shit ton of people hunting us right now.

Liam stops suddenly, his finger on his lips, telling me to be quiet. I stand completely still, biting my bottom lip, my hand over my heart. All I hear is dead silence and I look at Liam. The moon is bright tonight, but I can barely make out his expression.

Then I hear the sound of a stick breaking, and Liam charges just as a man comes into view. I stare wide eyed as Liam tackles the man to the ground, hitting him hard in the face. "Look away, Baby." I turn my head as I hear bones breaking.

When I turn back, the man is slumped over with his neck broken.

Liam walks back over to me and takes my hand, and we start running again. This goes on for what seems like forever; then he stops again. "You need to rest, Baby," he whispers.

I nod even though I am not sure he can see it. My legs feel like Jell-O.

He props me against the tree, unzips one of the backpacks, and pulls out a blanket. He wraps it around my back and hands me a bottle of water. He doesn't sit down. He is eyeing the woods around him, and I try to be as silent as possible. I open the bottle of water, and it hurts my hands because they are so cold. I take a sip and shut the bottle, and I pull the blanket tightly around me. Liam steps closer and sits down beside me, pulling me into his chest.

"Get warm, Baby, we have to move soon."

I close my eyes and soak in his warmth.

This is just awful. It is a disaster and I don't understand how they found us. This house is under a different name and is in no way associated with the club. We must have a leak, a leak who has been giving up our locations. I hit the panic button before we left. I hope the guys find us soon.

A branch snaps beside us, and Liam stands up. Then I hear someone running, and three guys pop into view. I stand up and ready my AK in a split second. Liam tackles two of them to the ground, and I shoot the other. Liam shoots the other two with his pistol.

"Liam, how about we do some fucking hunting?" I smile into the dark. I am tired of running, hiding, and watching my every move.

Let's bring the fun to them.

Liam grins at me and drops the backpacks, and together we head straight back in the direction we just left. Liam holds my hand until we reach a group of men. We come out from behind the tree and, together, we get rid of the threat that has been tracking us. They have been after our family, and they have threatened, stalked, and tried to kill us. I am so sick and tired of these fuckers.

Liam

The only reason I ran at all was because I wanted to make sure Paisley was safe. The moment she wanted to fight back, I was fucking proud.

There can't be many of these fuckers left between the Grim Sinners and us. We have been picking them off for a long time, and we must have killed around thirty tonight. I took out almost all of them myself, and she got the ones who tried to sneak up on us. This shit is part of life. Killing takes a bit of your soul, but it's you or them—and I can say it won't fucking be me.

Paisley has a bit of outlaw blood in her, and I can see she doesn't like it but she accepts this shit just like I do. We do whatever it takes to protect ourselves and our family. My best guess is that this is the last of these fuckers—this is their last hurrah.

We step out of the woods. She is holding my hand, and we walk through the field toward the house. Paisley's hand is like fucking ice. It's fucking cold outside, and I wish these fuckers had chosen another night to try this shit —when it's not thirty degrees outside.

We reach the house and someone steps out. I freeze in absolute fucking shock at the sight of the person standing in front of me. He raises his gun and pulls the trigger. I don't fucking move because I never expected to see this person again.

Dad.

Paisley

The very same man who tried to kidnap me is standing right on the front porch staring at Liam in pure disgust. Then he looks at me and raises his gun, and Liam doesn't move.

I raise my gun and shoot, not even bothering to aim. He pulls the trigger right after I shoot him, and he is hit on the forearm; it knocks the gun right out of his hand. He runs off the porch, and Liam just stares after the man, letting him get away. "Liam, what's wrong?"

He looks at me, and he doesn't look like the Liam I know. "That was my dad."

FUCK. Liam takes his hand out of mine, twisting his fingers through his hair. "I am going to fucking kill him! It was him threatening you! Was he the man in the van?" he asks, his voice shaking with anger.

"Yeah," I whisper.

Liam looks so pained at my answer, his eyes close and he swallows. "Baby, go in the house to the panic room. Lock the door tight. I am going to go find him." Liam kisses my forehead and runs off in the direction his dad went.

I close my eyes at the pain I feel because Liam is hurting so badly. I hate that his father has shown up all of these years later, just to fuck with him and me. He wanted to hit Liam right where it hurt, and I guess that was me. I rub my face and walk up the steps to the house. I open my eyes, and I am face-to-face with Liam's dad.

He smiles at me, looking way too much like Liam. My stomach churns.

"Night night."

From the corner of my eye, I spot a gun. It hits me hard on the side of the head. Everything goes black, and I feel my body hit the ground and tumble down the steps.

Liam

Where the fuck did he go? It's been thirty minutes. I'd better get back to Paisley.

I run back to the house. The first thing I see is her gun sitting on the front porch, the door wide open, and spots of blood on the steps. He took her and it's all my fault. My knees give out, and I hit the ground hard. My hands go to my face, trying to fucking control my anger.

That's when I hear the sound of bikes. I stand up and wait for my brothers. One by one they surround me. They turn off their bikes, and they all stare at me.

"There are thirty cartel members dead in those fucking woods." I point in the direction where I left them. "Then I found the person who was threatening Paisley."

I clench my jaw hard, trying not to fucking scream. I fucking hurt, I hurt so bad that she was taken from me and it was all my fault. "My fucking father, I went after him and he took her." I shake my head, looking at the ground, trying to fucking control myself. My heart is in fucking danger, and that shit is eating me up on the inside.

"She has a tracker in her ring," I tell Techy, who is already on his phone.

Her dad walks over to me and puts his hands on my shoulders. "Don't fucking blame yourself, you can't control everything, Liam. We will get her back, and we will make them suffer in the process."

I grin for the first time. They will pay. Oh, will they fucking pay. We can't fucking forget I was trained to kill some fuckers.

seventeen

Paisley

I wake up tied to a chair. My hands are tied behind me, but my legs are free. I look around at the house and immediately know it's abandoned. The windows are broken, the walls are graffitied, and the door is barely hanging from its hinges.

Men are talking in the next room. These fuckers are getting on my last nerve. Who the fuck do they think they are? They can't just continue kidnapping me and expect to get away with it.

Liam is going to blame himself for this. I know that he will never fully forgive himself, because he left me alone at the house, but he thought he was protecting me. It's not a situation we could have won. No matter what we did, the outcome wasn't guaranteed. We would never have guessed that Liam's father was planning all of this. I don't understand why. After all of these years, why now?

The broken-down door opens, and Liam's dad walks into the bedroom. He leans against the wall, staring down at me, and I hate that this fucker's face resembles Liam's. That makes me sick to my stomach. I hate this dumb fucker so much; I have never hated anyone like I do this person. I am looking into the eyes of the man who beat Liam and his sister. I am disgusted.

"I bet you're wondering why I have been gunning for you?" He tilts his head.

I don't say a word because, honestly, I don't give a fuck what the reason is. There is no excuse good enough for this dumb fucking person. I want to fucking beat him to within an inch of his life, over and over, because that is what he did to his kid. But that wouldn't be enough, because Liam and his sister bear the emotional scars.

"It seems that my son gave my wife money to run away from me a year ago, and I had to wait until he came home to settle the score. But I saw him with you and I got a much better idea. Why not kill you right in front of him?"

I just stare at him, not giving him any reaction. This man doesn't deserve anything. This man doesn't deserve to breathe. He is a pure piece of shit who needs to die.

Liam's dad walks over to the window. He looks at me and then back out the window. "Fuck, how did they find us already?"

I don't say a word. He doesn't know that I have a tracker in my engagement ring.

He punches the wall and charges over to me. He roughly pulls me out of the chair and drags me through the house, my arm wrenched up painfully, the gun pressed against my temple. He looks down at me like he is disgusted by my presence.

You're not the only one, fucker.

He throws the door open hard, and we are on the porch. Standing in the yard are Liam, Dad, and the other MC guys. Liam looks me up and down and I nod slightly, letting him know that I am okay. He takes his eyes off me, looking at his father head on. *That's my boy, show him what kind of person you are and that he means nothing to you.*

"Derek, what the fuck do you think you're doing?" Liam snarls, his voice unlike anything I've heard before.

Derek laughs loudly, like he is having the best time of his life. His breath brushes against my face, making me sick to my stomach, because the smell is unlike anything I have ever smelled before.

"You took something away from me, now I am here to do the same," Derek tells Liam, like he is doing the most normal and sane thing in the world.

Liam looks at him like he is the stupidest person in the entire world. "What are you talking about?"

Derek shifts me in his arms, and I can see that he is getting angrier. "Don't play these games, Liam. Stupid worthless fucker."

You know what? I am done with this shit. I raise my arm, grab the gun, and snap on the safety. Then I bring my head back, breaking his nose. He lets me go.

"You like to fucking beat on your kids? I am going to show you what worthless fuckers like you deserve!" I scream at him. I hurt for Liam and Braelyn and what this person did to them. Their father hit them and let them go hungry. This is me getting revenge. With all of my might, I kick the gun right out of his hand. It flies across the ground.

Derek looks at me, his face full of rage.

"Not such a badass, are you now?" I taunt him, smirking. He charges me, and I kick him hard in the balls. He hits the ground like a ton of bricks. I stand over him, bend down, and pound his face with my fist.

My heart, body, and soul are growing lighter with every second. I hate this person so much and have for years. Tears are falling down my face with every single hit. I scream and grab his hair and smash his head into the ground.

"Stupid fucker, I hate you so much for what you have done to him!" I scream and kick his side hard, his whole body curling into a ball, protecting himself.

A hand touches my shoulder, and I stop and turn around. Liam is standing beside me looking totally amused.

"Uhh, I don't think I needed rescuing," I mutter, and he throws his head back laughing at me and pulls me into his chest. I lay my head against his chest, closing my eyes, and relax for the first time since I went to sleep hours ago. This has been one hell of a night.

"Stupid bitch," Derek moans.

Liam lets me go and kicks him hard in the face. A tooth falls out of his mouth as he spits blood onto the ground. Dad comes over and takes me from Liam, pulling me away from the scene.

Liam

I bend down and look into the face of the person who made my life a living hell and enjoyed every second of it. Torch took Paisley and is going to take her away from this area until I've done what I need to do.

Derek stares at me with so much hate, and I will never fucking understand what made him this way. One day soon I want to be a dad, and I will do everything to love and protect my kid. This man isn't a fucking man but a pitiful excuse for a human being.

"Long time, fucker," I say. "Your fucking pain and misery ends here. This is where it stops, this is where I get my fucking peace. The shit that you tried to do didn't work."

I punch the ground by his face. I hate this person so fucking much. "Know that I am happy. I am going to marry the woman I have loved since I was seventeen years old, and I am going to have kids and they are going to have a good life." I smile. "Braelyn is married, she has two kids and she is a very successful and happy woman. We are fucking happy, and that is something you will never know."

Derek just fucking glares at me. "You took her away."

Then it fucking clicks. "You mean your wife? I gave her five hundred bucks, and she used that shit to leave your sorry ass. Good for her."

He tries to hit me in the face. I grab his fist and twist his arm, breaking it. "That will be the last time you will ever try to hit me, any last words?"

"Fuck you."

I laugh and take out my gun. "Fuck you too, piece of shit." I press the gun to his head, looking him dead in the eye, and pull the trigger. I close my eyes and stand up, and I turn around and look at my brothers. They are at my back, giving me support but giving me the space to do what I need to do.

"I need to call Ethan."

I step away and make the call. "You okay?" is the first thing out of his mouth.

"He is dead." I can hear him let out a deep breath.

"She can live in peace now," he whispers and I can hear his relief. Ethan hates him. He has been wanting to kill him for years, but that shit is hard to do when you're the chief of police. "Thank you, man." He hangs up and I put my phone back in my pocket.

Then I walk to Paisley. I need to fucking hold her and make sure that she is okay. That shit is hard to swallow; her being taken and the fear of what could have happened is a killer. She is my heart. She is an extension of me and she is mine. Now we can rest.

If only it were that easy.

eighteen

Two Months Later

"Harder!" I moan, gripping the counter hard. I am leaning over it with Liam pounding into me hard from behind.

"You want more, Baby?" he whispers into my ear, his breath making my whole body shiver.

"Yes, please," I beg. My body is on fire and just about over the edge, but I need a little more. A hand lands on my ass hard, then he lets loose and lets me have what I need. My whole body stiffens, my toes curl, and I brace myself.

His hand comes between me and the kitchen cabinet, his thumb and finger pinch my clit, and I come hard, my whole body shaking and my knees giving out. He keeps pounding into me, and I'm not even standing up at this point. His hands are gripping my waist, holding me up. I am complete Jell-O.

He comes a few seconds later, and he slowly and gently slips out of me and picks me up off the ground. He hugs me to him, and my head is resting on his chest as I try to catch my breath.

"What time do we have to be at dinner at the club?" I ask Liam, my eyes closed and my fingers running down his back.

"We have three hours." He kisses the side of my head. I hug him and let him carry me into the bathroom.

"We can have some more fun." I wink at him.

He laughs and we step into the shower. The next hour is filled with hot, steamy sex. Every single time is like the first time all over again, intense and just amazing.

We walk into the club, and I am so excited to see my family and friends. We haven't had a party like this in a while, and we used to have them all the time. The cartel has backed away. The presidents of our club and the Grim Sinners have signed a peace treaty and, for the first time in months, we can breathe easy. The moment the peace treaty was signed, the relief was something that is hard to describe. I can live with Liam and we don't have to constantly look over our shoulders anymore.

Liam's dad was after us—on top of the cartel, which was gunning for the women of the club. Between the two of them, it was an absolute mess for me. Liam's dad had a whole different agenda, but it overlapped and made it hard to figure out who was doing what.

I will never forget the moment we found out that it was Liam's father who was gunning for me, to make him pay for giving his wife the five hundred dollars she needed to get away from him. The bitch was just as guilty as he was for letting stuff happen to her daughter and Liam, but I also know living with a very manipulative man will have a huge effect on someone.

Working in the ER I see it every day. I see the faces of women who deal with abuse every single day because their men have them so confused and brainwashed they accept it. It's heartbreaking; no woman should have to feel the flesh of a man's fist on her face. Knowing what Liam had to deal with, I have been thinking a lot about adopting a kid and giving that child the life that I wish Liam had growing up. He had it good after Braelyn took him in, and I am beyond thankful for that. I want to do that for a kid. I want to give them everything that they have been missing.

Liam is standing next to me, holding my hand while he talks to the guys. I am so happy. I am blessed with so much in my life. I slip my hand free from Liam's and walk across the room to the food.

The door opens and a woman walks in. From this angle, it looks like the years haven't been good to her at all. I start to walk toward her. She puts her hand in her pocket and takes out a gun. She points the gun at someone, and my heart stops in my chest when I realize it's aimed at Liam.

I run, my heart pounding so hard. I tackle her hard from the side, right as the gun goes off. She hits the ground and the gun falls from her hand. I punch her hard in the face, and she groans and rolls over, holding her face. I look up at Liam to see him holding his shoulder. He was shot, stupid fucking bitch!

Shaylin runs over. "Don't let this bitch up," I tell her and run over to Liam. He is looking at the woman on the ground, and I touch his face to get his attention. "Baby, are you okay?"

He looks at me. "Yeah Baby, it was just a fucking graze. You saved my life." He pulls me into him and kisses my forehead. I let out a deep breath. I could have lost him. I was so close to losing him.

"Who is she, Liam?" I ask.

"That is Braelyn's mother, Derek's wife," he says, his voice completely devoid of emotion.

I am so angry. This woman is a worthless piece of shit. I look over at Kyle. "I want a room."

He grins at me, his arms across his chest. "You got it, baby girl."

"I am going to beat some ass," I tell him and he laughs. Then the doctor swoops in to check out Liam's shoulder.

Shaylin comes up beside me. Tyler is dragging Liam's stepmother back to the room, screaming and fighting, I smile at her and she starts cussing at me. One by one the ole ladies file in beside me: Shaylin, Jean, Myra, Chrystal, Alisha, and Kayla. These women will be with me, helping me do exactly what I need to do, and that is beating some ass.

The door slams shut behind me, and the women stand by my side. Tyler brought Liam's stepmother in, and she is hanging from the ceiling by her hands. I walk straight over to her and look into the face of the woman who fucked up so many lives. She may not have been the main abuser, but she let stuff happen.

"He killed him!" she screams, so loudly my ears are ringing.

"Of course he did! He was a fucking waste of space," I tell her straight out. I don't give two fucks.

Her eyes narrow on me, and she grips the chains above her head tighter. Her legs kick out toward me, and I laugh because it's pretty pathetic. Her stringy hair is in front of her face, which is covered with sores, dirt, and grime. Her clothes are covered in a bunch of stains, and a strange odor is coming from her. "He was a good man!" she screams in a shrill voice.

I look at her in absolute shock. "How was he a good man?"

She looks at the ground, and I can see that she is actually thinking about it. A minute later she looks at me. "He kept me from starving. I had a bed."

I hold my hands up in the air. "Well, excuse fucking me, he fed you and gave you a bed to sleep in. Was that in between him beating your kids and you?"

She sucks her lips into her mouth, her face getting redder with every single word. "Well, at least I am not an ugly, pathetic bitch like you."

I laugh because that was a pitiful attempt to get under my skin.

"I should have killed that stupid fucker when I had a chance, years ago, he should have never been born."

Red, that is what I see at her words. Something takes over my body, and I punch her hard in the mouth. I grab her jaw hard, getting right in her face. "How dare you say such a thing! He is the most amazing person, and you're a piece of shit that should have died years ago, you're nothing." I hate her too much. I don't understand how someone can be mean to their child, and I will never understand why this woman let it happen to Liam and Braelyn. She was just as guilty as he was. She needs to be buried right beside him in the fucking woods. Let her be in hell for eternity, because that is one thing I know for certain: she will be paying.

"So this bitch let someone hurt kids? Did I hear that correctly?" Shaylin is smiling that manic smile, holding a knife that is Butcher's. Shaylin is a badass bitch, a princess in the Grim Sinners club like I am a princess in the Devil Souls.

"I think we need to show this bitch what it's like to get their ass beat, since this bitch let her kids get the same treatment over the years," I tell the girls.

Then we let the bitch have it. We beat her ass, not caring that she is tied up and not able to fight back. Liam and Braelyn never had a chance to protect themselves. She should have done it.

Thirty minutes have passed, and her face is bloody, several teeth are missing, her jaw is lacerated, and a couple of fingers are broken.

She throws her head back, laughing. I step closer to her. What is she laughing at? That is only going to make me angrier. She looks at me, an evil smile on her face. "Please kill me and you will never know." She goes back to smiling, and my stomach twists.

I look at Kayla and see that she is just as confused. This is probably a ploy to get out of dying. That is something that is going to happen no matter what she says.

"Never know what?" I ask her, pretending to take the bait.

She smiles even wider and brings her face closer to me. I ignore the horrible smell coming from her mouth. "I had a baby eight years ago."

My heart hits the floor. Liam has a little brother or sister. She could be lying. I almost hope that she is because I hate the idea of another child having this kind of life.

"Boy or girl?"

"Boy." She cackles, and my stomach twists. I open the door and run into the main room to find Liam. He needs to know.

Liam sees me running and walks toward me, along with the other guys. He catches me, holding me by my elbows. "What is it?"

"She just told me that she had a baby eight years ago, a boy."

Liam's face pales and I can see that he has the same kind of mindset I did. It is a scary thing to think that another child is in that situation. His dad is dead but where is the kid?

Is there even a kid?

nineteen

Liam

I hope that she is lying, I hope that what she is saying is a bunch of shit to get out of dying and that I don't have a little brother who is suffering the same way I fucking did.

I follow Paisley into the interrogation room where Shaylin is breaking her fingers. "Tell me!" she screams and breaks her pinky finger. Shaylin looks at all of us and takes a step back, and Paisley does the same.

I walk straight to her, and she is staring at me. "You are going to tell me where the fuck he is or I will enjoy slicing every single inch of your skin off your body, then I will sew you back-to-fucking-together and do it over and over again. I will make you suffer and I will keep you alive for months," I snarl into her face, not giving a fuck that she is a woman. She is not a woman. She is a fucking piece of shit. I hate her more than my fucking father at this moment.

"Will you not kill me?"

"Not if you tell me where he is." I am lying right through my fucking teeth. She will be dead by the end of the day. She is just choosing how easy her death will be.

She tells us an address next. "His name is Caiden, he is eight years old." She stops and looks at my face like she is studying it. "You can't miss him because he looks just like you."

Fuck me.

I look at Kyle and he nods. "Let's roll!" he yells and everyone walks out of the room. I look at Paisley, who just looks sad. I bend and kiss her forehead. "I will be back, Baby." She nods and I follow my brothers.

I hope she is lying.

We find the address she gave us; it is a run-down drug house outside of town. We won't allow places like this to be in our town, and this is why it's just outside of our borders. We are all parked around this fucking house, and heads are sticking out of the windows and ducking back in.

It's fucking chaos inside. I can hear people running and shit slamming against the walls. Kyle raises his hand, giving us the go-ahead to get off our bikes and approach the house. I hear people running inside in pure panic. They are thinking we are here to shut them down and, honestly, we will probably also fucking clean this place out of drugs. That shit ruins lives.

I walk in front of everyone and kick the door in. Someone tries to run past me, and I grab him. "Is there a little boy here?" I ask him.

He looks like he is about to shit his pants, but he nods and points upstairs. I let him go and he runs away and climbs out of the house through a broken-out window.

I walk further into the house with Kyle and Torch on either side of me. I hope the fuck that this person imagined a kid.

I walk up the stairs, which are sinking with every step. This place is completely falling apart. I walk down the hallway and the brothers break off, searching each room. I go to the last room with Torch. I push the door open and there is a couple about to fucking shoot up right on the floor. They look up and see us. The girl screams, and I step away from the door as they run past. Torch walks to the bathroom and I check the closet. I open the door and look down.

Fuck me.

A pair of eyes identical to mine look back at me. I fall to the floor. "It's okay," I whisper softly. His body is shaking in fear. I notice how dirty and skinny he looks. This shit is not fucking fair. I hate that fucking bitch. "What is your name?" I ask him.

He looks at me, studying me, and I can tell that he is scared out of his mind. "Caiden," he says, barely above a whisper.

I close my eyes, tilt my head to the side, and try to hide how fucking angry I am. I had a brother that I never knew about. I let out a deep breath, trying to relax my body so I don't look so mean. "I'm Liam, nice to meet you." I stick my hand out, and he looks at it; then he slowly lifts his hand and shakes mine. I smile widely. "I just found out, Caiden, that I'm your brother and I came here for you."

His eyes widen, and he stares at me like I just told him the sky was black. "We have the same eyes."

I nod. "Yes, we do, we look a lot alike."

He moves a little closer, looking at me more intently.

"How come I never saw you before?" he asks, and I notice that his body isn't shaking as hard.

I sit down on the floor. "I never knew about you until an hour ago, and once I found out I came straight here to take you away from this place and this life."

"Take me where?" he whispers. He looks down at his hands, breaking my heart.

"My home, you will have your own bed, toys, you can go to school and you can be a kid. You will never have to worry about being hungry again."

He looks up at me, and his eyes are filled with tears. He blinks and they fall down his face. "You won't hit me?"

FUCK.

I grit my teeth, trying to stop myself from punching the wall. I hate that the fucker died that night. I wish I he were still here so I could torture him over and over.

"I will never hit or hurt you in any way, nor will I let someone else hurt you. Never again," I tell him. He watches me, and it's like he is making sure that I am being truthful.

He slowly nods, and I hold out my hand. He puts his hand in mine, and I stand up and pull him with me gently. I turn around and see my brothers standing at my back, watching everything going down. "Caiden, these are your uncles," I tell him quickly so he is not scared.

He looks at all of them but moves closer to my side. I tighten my hand around his, and I lead him out of the room. We walk through the house with people watching us leave.

"Don't get too comfortable," Kyle tells them and I grin. He had the exact same thought I did. This place needs to be burned to the ground. Caiden was hiding in a closet; he had to have been absolutely terrified. She left him here, and she knew she probably wouldn't come back.

After stepping outside the house, I take him straight to my bike. "I am going to put you on in front of me." He looks at the bike, and I take that moment to get a really good look at him now that we're in the sunlight.

He looks just like me. We have the same hair and eye color, and our facial features are a lot alike. He is way too skinny; he has not had it easy. I hate this so fucking much. I hate that he had this kind of life when I could have given him something so much different.

I take out my phone and call Paisley, and she answers almost instantly. "You have him?"

"Yeah Baby, can you bring the basics for him?" I ask her. I want to get to our house and just let him get used to me and Paisley. "You don't mind him living with us?"

"Fuck no, I want him to live with us so I can spoil him and make sure he has a good life."

That's my woman.

I climb on my bike and help him on in front of me. I take out a small leather jacket that's Paisley's, and I wrap it around him so he doesn't get cold. "Ready?"

He nods and I start the bike.

Then we head home.

twenty

Paisley

I hate that she wasn't lying and there was a little boy. I have spent the last hour getting everything I possibly can. I got Kayla to help me because my little brother is around his age. I called Liam a few minutes ago, and he told me that Braelyn offered to take him in but Liam wanted to be the one to take care of him.

He also wanted to make sure that I was okay with it, and I am. The idea of adopting a kid has been on my mind a lot lately. I pull up in front of the house, the gate shutting behind me, and I let out a deep breath. My eyes close because this is a big deal, and I want everything to go perfectly. I reach over into the passenger seat and grab the bags. I got a couple of days' worth of clothes, including underwear and pajamas.

I step out of the car and walk up to the front porch. The door opens the moment I touch the doorknob. Liam is standing in the entrance, and he takes the bags from me. I barely notice. I just look at his face, making sure that he is okay. "You okay?" I whisper and he nods, smiling slightly, and I can tell instantly that he has been affected by all this. He steps back and I take my shoes off, tossing them by the door.

"Where is he?" I say softly. I don't want him to be scared.

"He is in the living room. I'm about to take the burgers off the grill. I asked him what is one thing that he is craving, and he wants burgers." He smiles slightly. "He looks just like me." I smile back and take his hand, and we walk together into the living room. Sitting on the couch is a smaller version of Liam, there is no doubt about that.

Another thing I notice is that he is small, way too small for an eight-year-old boy, and he is dirty in a way that shows he has been living in a rough situation for a while. "Caiden, this is Paisley, my fiancé. Paisley, this is Caiden."

I pull my hand free from Liam's and slowly walk over to him. He watches me wearily, and I bend down in front of him, putting him at eye level with me. "It's very nice to meet you." I smile widely and lift my hand for him to take. He takes his eyes off my face then looks at my hand and then back at my face, like he is trying to see if I really want him to shake my hand. I hate that bitch more and more. He is making sure that this isn't a test or something.

He slowly lifts his hand and places it in mine.

"It's so nice to meet you," I say again, smiling.

He ducks his head, not before I see his small smile. I look back at Liam and smile.

"I got you some things until I can take you shopping."

Liam walks over and hands me the bags, and I set them on the couch by him. He looks at the bags like they are going to pop up and bite him. My throat thickens at the sight of his shocked face.

"This is mine?"

"Yes, it's just a few things until I can take you shopping and get whatever else you need and want," I tell him and push the bags closer. He smiles at me, and my heart stops in my chest because he looks just like Liam. He grabs one of the bags and starts taking out the clothes. He touches the shirts. It's like he can't believe it's real. He looks at every single item, his eyes wide. My heart feels like it's shattered into a million pieces because a little thing like clothes has him so happy and shocked.

I hate her, I hate him. I hate them so much because this precious little boy had the life he did. He was found in a fucking drug house in a closet. I don't even want to know what might have happened to him and the things he has seen. And he went without simple things like food, a bed, clothes and, most of all, someone to love him.

There is still one bag left. It was on sale and I couldn't resist getting it for him. Liam used to talk about how Braelyn got him an Xbox, and that was the first gift he'd ever received. I just wanted to get Caiden something special, and he'll have something to do when he goes to bed tonight.

"I have one more thing for you." I look over at Liam, who is still leaning against the wall. I reach inside the bag and take out a Nintendo DS and a game. I set it on Caiden's lap, and he stares at it in absolute shock.

"This is for me?" he whispers, touching the shrink wrap around the box.

"Of course. I wanted you to have something that is yours that'll help you kill some time."

I play it cool. He doesn't look at me, and I can tell that he is crying. I stand up and walk across the room to Liam, and he pulls me into his arms and hugs me. "That was sweet, Baby, he hasn't had a lot of good in his life. Braelyn did something similar for me," he whispers softly enough that only I can hear. I kiss his cheek and look back at Caiden, who is still staring down at his game.

"Ready to eat?" Liam asks him and Caiden looks at him, seeming unsure.

"Want to eat here in the living room? We can watch some TV and relax," I offer, and he relaxes slightly. "There is a bathroom right through there. Go wash up and I will bring the food in here."

I walk into the kitchen to help Liam, and he is putting all the burgers on a plate. I walk to the fridge and grab a couple of sodas along with some water.

"Do you know how he likes his burgers?" I ask Liam.

"Yeah, he just likes plain cheeseburgers."

I walk to the cabinet and grab three plates and some napkins. I put some fries on the plates, carry them into the living room, and set them on the coffee table.

Liam sets the huge stack of burgers on the table and, a second later, Caiden walks back into the living room. I sit down on the couch, and Caiden slowly walks over and sits down beside me. I hand him a plate and put two burgers on it. Liam sits down on the other side and turns on a new kid's movie. I hide my smile and dig into my food with Liam.

Liam

It fucking kills me that he is starving. In minutes he has demolished his entire plate. Paisley is hiding her face, and I can tell that she is hurting. I am mad—no, I am pissed. I want to kill someone. I want to make someone suffer because I know exactly how he is feeling because I was him.

Caiden has finished his food. "Eat all you want, there is plenty more," I urge him and he looks at me, unsure. I head in the direction of the food. He stands up and takes two more burgers. Paisley looks at me, and I can see the unshed fucking tears in her eyes.

Fuck me, today has been a mess. My stepmother tried to kill me, and then she let us know that I had a brother.

I am thankful that she said something because if she hadn't, I would never have known. Braelyn offered to take him in, but I wanted to do this. I wanted to give him a life. Braelyn did that for me, and I want to do the same for him. I'm glad that he is young enough that he won't remember a lot of his childhood, or I hope he doesn't.

It's fucking eerie how much he looks like me. Caiden and I both look a lot like my dad. Braelyn looks a lot like her mother—what she would look like if she weren't on drugs and hadn't been through years of beatings. I saw a picture of her when she was young, and she and Brae could be twins.

It's fucking crazy how someone can start out somewhat normal, but then it all changes when they meet someone who takes over their life, and not for the better. They change, they let stuff slide, and then everything they once were is gone. Brainwashing in abusive relationships is a real thing. It molds the brain until a person becomes someone they never wanted to be.

I look over at Caiden, who is concentrating on his food. I make a promise, in this moment, to give him a life that I never had. I want him to have that. I will make it my fucking mission.

That is a promise.

Paisley

I look at the clock on the wall, and it's nine o'clock. We just got finished eating a little while ago. "Caiden, ready to hit the showers and go to sleep?" I know he has to be exhausted; his eyes are drooping.

"Okay," he says and stands up. Liam picks up his bags. Caiden grabs his Nintendo DS, holding it close to his body. Liam walks in front of us, and I stay close to Caiden's side, hoping that I can comfort him even if it's just a little bit.

Liam pushes open a bedroom door near ours. "You have your own bathroom," I tell him, and Liam sets his bags on his bed. "On the table is a controller to the TV, you can relax before you sleep tonight." I just want him to be happy and feel relaxed, and I think he needs some alone time to get his bearings and wrap his head around everything that's happened. I don't know what to do besides trying to make sure that he is comfortable. "We will be in the living room, yell if you need something." I smile and touch the top of his head. He smiles slightly and looks down at the ground. He is too cute.

Liam takes my hand and we walk into the living room. I sit down on the couch, utterly exhausted, and Liam sits down beside me. He looks at the coffee table, staring into space, and I can tell that he is just as exhausted as I am. I lean over, laying my head against his shoulder. "I am so sorry, Liam," I whisper, my nose stinging from unshed tears.

"I hate it, Baby, so fucking much." He slides onto the floor then turns around and lays his face on my lap, his hands holding onto my hips.

I bend down and kiss the back of his head, my fingers stroking his hair. "I am so sorry, Baby, so sorry. I will help you with everything, through it all."

He nods his head, which is still in my lap.

"I love you so fucking much, Baby," he says, looking up at me.

I put my hands on either side of his face. "I love you too, my Liam."

He smiles and pulls me down, hugging me. I lay my head on his shoulder and, for the first time in hours, I relax. It's amazing that, from someone's touch alone, I can feel such peace. A few minutes later he stands up, taking me with him, and we lie down on the couch.

I continue stroking Liam's arm and his head. I can't help but worry about him. I hate the fact that he had such a rough go of it, and now he's learned that his brother has been living the life he used to live. He could have helped if he had known; he could have taken Caiden out of the situation sooner. That is enough to drive anyone crazy, and I know that it's eating him up because he's a very protective guy.

Thirty minutes later, I hear a door opening and I open my eyes. Caiden walks into the living room in his new pajamas looking so cute! I can't get over how much he looks like Liam.

"You ready for bed, bud?" Liam asks, sitting up and pulling me with him.

Caiden looks around the room, his arms across his chest. "Yeah, I think so."

"Want me to tuck you in?" Liam asks, scooting closer to the edge of the couch.

Caiden looks at Liam like he has grown two heads. "What's that?"

My heart shatters right then and there. Liam leans back into the couch, and I can tell that he is just as shocked. It's heartbreaking that he doesn't even know what tucking someone in is. He has never had that and that's so sad.

"I will show you," Liam says, his voice rough with emotion. Liam walks over to him, putting his hand on the back of his head. Caiden's hair is wet from the shower. I follow him, just watching. I lean against the doorframe, and Liam helps him onto the bed.

"Want me to read you a book?" Liam asks him. Caiden slowly nods his head. I can tell that he is totally reeling from everything going on. Liam takes out his phone and sits down on the bed with him.

Caiden scoots over and looks at Liam. Liam reads him a story, and Caiden never takes his eyes off Liam the whole time. I sit down in the doorway, and I just fall more and more in love with Liam. I am just getting a glimpse of what kind of father he could be, and I have a strong feeling he will become a dad to this little boy.

A few minutes later Liam finishes the story. Caiden's eyes are closed. Liam slowly slides off the bed and pulls the covers up to Caiden's neck. "Goodnight," Liam whispers and I push myself to my feet.

Liam walks over to me, looking back one more time, and Caiden's eyes are still closed. I walk out of the bedroom. Liam turns off the light and pulls the door halfway closed so the light from the hallway can give him some light.

Liam and I walk into our bedroom, two rooms down from his. Liam closes the door behind us, and I sit on the edge of the couch, exhausted.

Liam looks at me. "Tired, Baby?" he asks me.

"Exhausted," I admit. I run my hands over my face. Sitting on the floor watching Liam and Caiden made me so sleepy I could have slept right there.

Liam walks into the bathroom and comes back, a minute later, with my makeup remover and some cotton balls. He sits down on the bed beside me then opens the bottle.

"You're so sweet, Baby." I kiss his cheek and he smiles, showing me that dimple.

I close my eyes and let him take off all my makeup, getting sleepier by the second. Today has been a long day on top of being so emotionally draining. "You sure you don't mind him being here?" Liam asks.

I open my eyes and look at him. "Not at all, Liam, I would honestly love to adopt him. He is family and family stays with family, no matter what."

Liam smiles, shaking his head. "How did I get so fucking lucky with you?"

I smile back. "I think the same thing about you, Baby." I touch his cheek and lean forward, hugging him.

"Come on, Baby, let's change and go to sleep." He yawns and stands up, walks to our closet, and throws me a shirt and a pair of shorts

I change clothes, and I already feel much better after getting out of my tight jeans and this bra. There is no better feeling than taking your bra off after a long day.

I climb into bed, pulling back the covers and slipping between the sheets, and I sigh loudly. Liam comes out of the closet a second later in a pair of shorts.

He falls into bed beside me then turns over, pulling my back to his front. "What a fucking day, good night, Baby," he grumbles and I close my eyes, letting sleep take me.

Paisley

I wake up and look at the clock by the bed, and it shows it's eight o'clock. I peek over my shoulder at Liam and see that he is still in a deep sleep. I need to get up and check on Caiden.

I slowly slip out from under Liam's arm. Usually every time I move in my sleep he wakes up and pulls me back to him. Since he didn't do that, he must be exhausted.

I pad across the room and to Caiden's room, and he is sitting up in bed looking into the hallway.

"Want some breakfast?" I whisper and he climbs out of bed and walks to me. I smile at him and he lowers his head, blushing. I turn away and, together, we start toward the kitchen.

I feel a hand touching mine, and I look down and see that he is trying to hold my hand. I open my hand, and he slips his hand into mine.

"What do you want for breakfast?"

"Cinnamon rolls?" he whispers.

"Anything you want, honey," I tell him and, together, we walk into the kitchen. "Want to sit here or do you want to help me?"

He fully smiles for the first time since I met him yesterday, and I almost fall on my ass right there because of how much, once again, he reminds me of Liam. "I would like to help you, Paisley." Be still my heart! He is so cute.

I get him a little stool to stand on so he can reach the tabletop, and I hand him a bowl and some eggs. "Crack these eggs in here, then use this to whisk them." He eagerly takes an egg, barely tapping it on the counter.

Liam

I walk downstairs and the sight before me is something I want to see for the rest of my life. Paisley and Caiden are laughing, having the time of their lives cooking together.

I woke up worried about Caiden and I know now, in this moment, that everything will be okay.

"Good morning!"

Paisley and Caiden look at me, and Paisley smiles that smile that fucks with my heart every single time. Caiden smiles at me too.

"You know, I think today we should go shopping," I tell Caiden pointedly, and he tries to play it cool, going back to putting icing on the cinnamon rolls.

Paisley smooths down the back of his hair. "We have to get stuff for your room."

He looks up at Paisley. "My room? I am going to be living here? With you guys?" He looks genuinely shocked.

"Yes, you will be living here with us."

"What happened to Mommy?" he says, and I can tell that he is sad.

FUCK.

Paisley looks at me, panicked. What the fuck do I say to that?

"She left me, didn't she?" he says sadly.

I don't know what to fucking say or do, and I also don't want to lie. I bend down so I am face-to-face with him. I put my hand on his arm to get his attention.

"Do you want to live with your mommy?"

He shakes his head. "I don't want to stay with her anymore, I like it here." His body starts shaking under my hand.

"You're not going anywhere, and you will be living with us forever. Your mommy decided to give you a better life and let you stay with us," I say.

He relaxes. "Okay, I would like to stay here." He looks at me and hugs me.

I close my eyes, hugging him back tightly. His little arms squeeze me with all of his might. Someone touches my side and, when I open my eyes, Paisley is standing beside us with tears falling down her face.

"Can I have my cinnamon rolls now?" His voice is muffled against my shoulder. I laugh and set him back down on the floor.

Paisley leans down and gives him a quick hug. He hugs her back with a smile on his face. I am fucking glad that he is getting comfortable with us. I hope that the shit he had to deal with before leaves his life completely. I want him to have good memories, like making breakfast with Paisley.

Paisley helps him fix his plate and he carries it to the dining room table; I grab mine and hers. We all sit down together digging into our food. "Are you guys married?" he asks, his face covered in icing.

"Not yet." I wink at Paisley, and she blushes and looks down at her plate, smiling wide. A bell rings in the house, letting me know someone is at the gate. "I forgot Braelyn was coming." I stand up and walk to the iPad hanging from the wall. The video shows it's Braelyn and Ethan. I push the button unlocking the house and the gate, letting them in. I turn around and notice that he looks nervous.

"Braelyn is your sister and mine," I tell him and he kind of relaxes.

He scoots his plate across the table. It's empty. "Do you want more?" Paisley asks him and he shakes his head. I can tell that he is nervous.

Braelyn walks into the dining room and looks straight at Caiden, then at me. "He looks just like you."

I laugh because it's true.

Caiden is staring at Braelyn. "You look like Mommy," he says; then he stands up and walks over to her.

She bends down and hugs him. "Yes, I do. I'm your sister Braelyn."

"I'm Caiden." He smiles at her.

Braelyn looks at me. "We found a box of yours at the house and brought it to you, Liam." Ethan sets the box down on the table.

"We are going shopping in a little bit, Braelyn, if you want to go with us," Paisley says.

Braelyn nods immediately. "I would love to go."

A little bit later they leave, leaving me and Ethan alone. "She still alive?" he asks about Caiden and Braelyn's mom.

"For now," I tell him straight out. I don't care if he is the chief of police. First and foremost, he is family and he hates the bitch just like I do.

He has firsthand knowledge of what our childhood was like. Braelyn lived that life until she was eighteen and went off to college, but her troubles didn't end there. I can't even stand the thought of what she went through.

Ethan saved her. He took her right off the streets and made her realize that she is more than the life she was dealt. Then he took me in and treated me like I was his son, even though I was practically grown. Although I was seventeen years old, in a sense, I was a kid. He made me into the man I am today, with the MC helping mold me.

Paisley was another huge influence on my life. I knew that I wanted her, and I did everything I could to be the man that would deserve her.

"I have a proposition for you."

I lean against the counter. "What's that?"

"Let me put her in jail for the rest of her life. She won't ever get out but, this way, if Caiden ever wants to see her again, it will be an option. I have connections with a judge."

I think on it. She tried to kill me, and she put this little boy through hell. Left him in a fucking drug house, where anything could have happened to him. But I understand the part about Caiden wanting to see her later in life.

I am not in the business of hurting women. I can't even fathom hurting one, even though she is a bitch who doesn't deserve mercy. "I will talk to the club," I tell him. Ethan nods.

"How are Xavier and Samantha?"

He grins. "Samantha is a mini Braelyn, but she has a temper on her that is all me. Xavier is fucking smart and has it in his head that he is going to be a vet." His face grows serious. "He came out to me that he is gay, and he was fucking terrified. I hate that he felt that I would look at him differently."

Fuck me, I've known Xavier was gay for a while, but I am glad he finally came out to Ethan.

"I love him and who the fuck cares if he likes boys? I just want him happy."

"I found out a long time ago. I knew he was worried, but I told him he had nothing to worry about. You're a fucking good dad, man, I want to thank you for taking me in all those years ago."

"Don't make me fucking emotional, Liam, I can't handle that shit." His voice cracks and I laugh.

"Want a beer?" I ask him and he nods, the subject over.

Paisley

Hours Later

After many hours of shopping, we've gotten just about everything he could possibly need. He has had a blast. He was bursting at the seams and laughing, having the time of his life. That was the most amazing part: seeing him let himself go, quit overthinking his every move, and be a kid.

It's around eleven o'clock at night. Caiden is in bed asleep, and I am putting everything away. We also went grocery shopping because I wanted to make sure we have things he likes.

I want to spoil him. I know that he's never had much. The clothes he wore to our house the first time were so worn out they were paper thin and on the verge of falling apart.

"Liam, want to go through your things Braelyn brought?" I ask him. He is finishing putting stuff away in cabinets in the kitchen.

"Yeah, Baby." He shuts the cabinet door and walks over to me. I open the box and the first thing I see is a pair of shoes.

Liam reaches in and takes out the shoes. "Holy fuck, these are the shoes I wore to Braelyn's. And my clothes, along with the few things I had at the time."

I stare at the fucking shoe, with a hole in the front where his toe would be. Tears fill my eyes for the tenth time in the past two days.

Liam looks at me. "Why are you crying, Baby." He reaches over and catches a tear.

I look at the shoe and back at him. "The shoe, it's sad that you wore a shoe with a hole in it."

His face softens, and he throws the shoe in the box and pulls me into his arms. "Baby, that is not my life anymore. It's just a fucking shoe." He kisses my forehead, running his fingers through my hair.

I sniff loudly. "I know it's just a shoe, but—meeting Caiden, then seeing the shoe—it hit me again how hard you had it."

His hand slides down my back and he squeezes my ass.

"I am trying to be sad here, Liam," I tease and he squeezes again.

I lift my hand off his back, smacking his ass.

"I don't want you sad, Baby," he tells me through his laughter, and I bury my face in his neck, nipping at his throat to make him laugh harder because he is ticklish there.

He grabs my hands and puts me on the table. I smile at him. I am so happy. I am blessed to have someone like him.

He smiles down at me, his hands on either side of my face.

"I love you, Liam, so much."

He smiles wider, his dimple popping out. "I love you too, Paisley, you have given me a life that I never thought was possible. You're my whole fucking world and have been for years. I thought for years about how it would be if we were together, but I never expected this. You're beyond my expectations."

Don't cry, I chant over and over in my head, but I am not sure that I can hold it in. He is the sweetest person on this earth, and he is mine.

My Liam.

Caiden

I watch Liam and Paisley, and I wipe the tears off my face because, for the first time ever, I have a family.

A family.

The family that I have always wanted.

I look up at the ceiling. *Thank you.*

epilogue

Wedding Day

"Baby, just move back in with me and be my little girl forever," Dad pleads with me for the tenth time since we got up this morning. He and Caiden stayed in the room with me while I was getting my hair and makeup done.

Caiden and I have become really close. Honestly, I think of him as my son, and he accidentally calls me Mom sometimes. He makes the same mistake with Liam. I wouldn't mind him being mine. In my heart he is my little boy, and I know Liam feels the same way.

"Daddy, we've gone over this," I tell him, rolling my eyes.

He glares at me, his arms across his chest. He is leaning against the door, and I know he is doing that on purpose. "Apparently not fucking enough, because you are getting married today."

I laugh out loud because he looks like he is in pain.

"I hope that you have a baby soon so I can have someone to play with," Caiden says.

My father turns as pale as a ghost. "You don't have babies." He grips the wall.

"I will probably have a few," I tell him.

My father gives me the meanest look I have ever seen directed toward me, and Caiden grips my hand and steps up closer to him.

Caiden has been around Liam a lot. Liam is protective and it's been wearing off on Caiden. If we are out alone, he sticks right by my side the whole time. He has come a long way. In the beginning any loud or sudden movements made him nervous. You can't wake him up abruptly because it scares him. We noticed that he would hide food in his room, a habit from years of not having enough to eat.

He is in school and he is playing baseball. He is scary good at it. He'd never played before, until he asked to try out. When he has a game, an entire stand is ours because so many people show up. It's hilarious seeing the looks we get when we get so into the game, even though it's just little kids playing.

The door is opening, and it hits Dad's back. He turns around to see Kayla looking through the crack. He steps back and she walks in. "It's time." She smiles widely.

"No, it's not!" Dad says loudly and I can't help but laugh.

"Come on, Daddy." I stand up, and Kayla comes over and takes off the sheet that I had wrapped around my dress while I was getting my makeup and hair done. I love my dress. It's a mermaid-style dress. It's body hugging until it gets to my thighs, where it flares out. It has a heart-shaped top with lace down to my elbows.

My hair is in long barrel waves, and it's pinned up on one side. Brittany did an amazing job. She is a princess of the Grim Sinners, like Shaylin, and she is the best makeup and hair stylist in Texas.

Caiden puts his hand in mine and, together, we walk to the entrance of the main room, where Liam is waiting. I stand out of sight watching all of my groomsmen and bridesmaids walk down the aisle.

Liam's best man is Tyler, and we have almost all of the MC guys as his groomsmen. I have a lot of the ole ladies as bridesmaids.

Kayla has been absolutely amazing the whole time I was planning the wedding. Over the years I have come to think of her as my mother. My dad married her when I was nineteen, and she was the best thing to ever happen to him. He was the best thing that happened to her too. She had nobody in life until him, and he gave her something she has always wanted. Family.

Caiden walks out with the rings and the doors shut. Dad is standing across the room.

"Come on, Daddy."

He stares at me for a few seconds then shakes his head and approaches me. "Why do you have to get married, Angel? When did you grow up?" His voice cracks.

"Daddy, don't make me cry." My voice cracks and he pulls me over, hugging me. He kisses the top of my head, and I grip his suit.

I love my daddy so much. He is my best friend, and I have been blessed to have a father who has done everything he's done for me. "I love you, my baby," he says softly. The music starts playing.

"I love you too," I whisper and the door opens, revealing the packed church and my Liam. I smile and he smiles back at me, and every single person in the room disappears, leaving Liam and me,

Mr. and Mrs. Beckham.

A Couple of Months Later

Christmas Morning

This is Caiden's first Christmas with us, and Liam and I are really excited as we sit on the couch waiting for him to wake up. I have a huge surprise for Liam, one that he won't expect.

A minute or so later I hear Caiden running. Liam and I sit up, waiting for him to come into the room. Caiden skids to a stop and looks at the presents on the floor.

"Merry Christmas, Caiden!" I tell him and he runs over to hug me and Liam. "Ready to open your presents?" I ask him, and he nods so fast his whole body is shaking. I laugh and motion for him to go for it.

Liam and I have our presents separated so that Caiden can just open all of his. He sits down on the floor. His hair is messed up on top. The last time I took him to get a haircut, he wanted the same style as Liam. He and Liam have become like best friends. Liam bought him a mini-Harley, and he never wants to get off it. My heart is about to burst with fear every time he gets on it. I will have gray hair before I get to thirty years old.

Caiden finishes opening his presents and crawls under the tree. He comes out with an envelope in his hand. I look at Liam, confused, but he just smiles. I guess he is in on it.

Caiden walks over to me. "I have something for you." He sets the envelope on my lap. I smile at him. I slowly open it, pulling out the papers inside.

My stomach twists at the sight of the words: "Adoption of Caiden." My eyes fill with tears, and I look at Caiden. "You want me to adopt you?" My voice is shaking along with my hands, and Liam touches my back.

Liam has already adopted him, but we weren't married yet. "I want you to be my mommy." Well, fuck. I set the papers on the coffee table and pull Caiden to me, hugging him. I couldn't stop the tears even if I wanted to. "I want nothing more, Baby." Liam never once takes his hand off my back.

"Okay," he whispers and hugs me tighter.

A few minutes later, I manage to compose myself, but I can't bring myself to let him go. This little boy is so precious. He took over my heart the moment I met him, and it's only grown.

"You have gotten your wish," I whisper into his ear. He pulls back and looks at me, smiling. He has asked me over and over, since Liam and I got married, when I was going to have a baby.

I am pregnant.

Twelve weeks to be exact. It totally slipped my mind that it was time for my contraceptive injection.

"Really?" He grins happily and I nod my head, grinning, I reach behind me and hand Liam the small package.

Liam looks at both of us, confused. "What am I missing?" he says.

"Open it," I tell him and he looks at the package, then back at us again. He opens the package achingly slowly, and it's killing me.

He finally gets the wrapping off, after what seems like forever, and opens the box. I put the pregnancy test on top of the sonogram pictures of the baby. I thought I could be pregnant, but I wanted to be sure and I wanted to wait until Christmas to tell him.

Liam doesn't say a word for a few beats, just staring down into the box, and then he looks at me. "You're pregnant?" he says softly.

I touch his cheek. "I'm twelve weeks."

He sets the box on the coffee table then gently lifts me onto his lap and hugs me, his hand resting on my stomach. Caiden hugs both of us. "I can't believe that you're pregnant." He kisses my cheek.

"Yes, we are." I smile at Caiden, who looks so excited. He puts his hand on my stomach, right beside Liam's.

My life is just perfect. The cartel has completely left, and we have been at peace ever since they disappeared. The cartel made everyone realize how fragile life is, how easily everything could have been taken away. The club is finding and testing new ways to keep everyone protected and make everything safer for all of us.

If it weren't for our protected vehicles, we wouldn't be alive because we have been shot at so many times. If the glass weren't bulletproof, we have been shot multiple times over.

The Grim Sinners and Devil Souls found a private school right between the two clubs, and they decided to send their kids there because it's smaller, safer, and easily manipulated with money so we can protect it better. The cartel has left everyone weary and looking over our shoulders for the unexpected, and they don't want to take a chance with the kids.

"I think it's a girl." Caiden says, interrupting my thoughts.

Liam freezes and he looks horrified. "No, it's fucking not."

I laugh loudly. It's already starting.

A Few Months Later

"Congrats, you guys, it's a girl!" the doctor says during my sonogram to determine the gender of our baby, and Liam's body sinks, a look of pure panic on his face.

Dad bursts out laughing. "I am going to enjoy every second of this. She is going to find a fucker just like you, Liam. Prepare yourself."

Liam looks at my dad with absolute hatred. "No, she fucking isn't!" he snarls and looks like he is about to punch my dad right in the face.

"Oh yes she is," Dad says through laughing. He is bent over, holding his stomach.

"She is never going to get married, she is never going to do anything like that." Liam puts his hand softly on my stomach. "She is my angel."

Dad sinks into the chair, laughing even harder.

Oh, how much he came to eat his words. She found herself a Liam: the vice president of the Grim Sinners, Mason.

Oh boy.

THE END

acknowledgements

To my readers, thank you so so so much from the bottom of my heart! You guys are the best! Without you guys I wouldn't be here today. <3

Lydia, my wonderful publicist and PA, thank you for everything you do for me! I would be lost if you wasn't around to keep me sane! AKA Boss Lady!

My Review Team and my Reader Groups: You guys are my biggest support system and push me to be better with every book. You also never hesitate to give me words of encouragement.

about the author

LeAnn Asher's is a blogger turned author who released her debut novel early 2016 and can't wait to see where this new adventure takes her. LeAnn writes about strong-minded females and strong protective males who love their women unconditionally.

Website: https://authorleannashers.com
Facebook: https://www.facebook.com/LeAnnashers
Instagram: https://www.instagram.com/leann_ashers/
Twitter: https://twitter.com/LeannAshers
Goodreads:
https://www.goodreads.com/author/show/14733196.LeA
nn_Ashers
Amazon: https://www.amazon.com/LeAnn-
Ashers/e/B01AVUCOLG

More from LeAnn Ashers

Forever Series

Protecting His Forever
Loving His Forever

LeAnn Ashers

Devil Souls MC Series

Torch
Techy
Butcher
Liam

Grim Sinners MC Series

Lane
Wilder